P9-DEC-006

Scribble

Scribble

Richard W. Jennings

Houghton Mifflin Company Boston 2004

Walter Lorraine Books

Walter Lorraine (wr) Books

Copyright © 2004 by Richard W. Jennings

All rights reserved. For information about permission
to reproduce selections from this book, write to Permissions,
Houghton Mifflin Company, 215 Park Avenue South,
New York, New York 10003.

www.houghtonmifflinbooks.com

Library of Congress Cataloging-in-Publication Data
Jennings, Richard W. (Richard Walker), 1945-
  Scribble / Richard W. Jennings.
     p. cm.
  "Walter Lorraine Books."
  Summary: With only his dog Scribble for companionship, a twelve-
year-old boy mourns the death of his best friend and tries to under-
stand the meaning of strange, otherworldly visitations from the likes
of Sam Walton and Nat "King" Cole.
  ISBN 0-618-43367-8
  [1. Dogs—Fiction. 2. Ghosts—Fiction. 3. Grief—Fiction. 4.
Friendship—Fiction.] I. Title.
  PZ7.J4298765Sc 2004
  [Fic]—dc22

                                                          2004000736

ISBN–13: 978-0-618-41058-3

Printed in the United States of America
MP 10 9 8 7 6 5 4 3 2 1

Acknowledgments

My sincere thanks to the Kansas Arts Commission for its significant contribution toward the completion of this book; to Walter Lorraine, my long-suffering editor at Houghton Mifflin, and Stacy Graham, his gifted assistant and my phone friend, for daring to shepherd yet another "quirky" project; to George Nicholson and Paul Rodeen at Sterling Lord Literistic, for their suggestions, encouragement, and financial intervention; and to Marc Jaffe— no writer ever had a better friend in the business, or anywhere else, for that matter; and, finally, to Eddie Tomorrow, the Jack Russell terrier who adopted me at just the right time.

RWJ Overland Park, Kansas 2004

In Memoriam
James J. Johnston

Scribble

Where to Begin?

On the one hand, if it weren't for my dog, I might have lived my whole life without ever seeing the spirits who walk among us, if *walk* is the right word for what these disembodied beings do. On the other hand, the dawning of my teen years might have gone a little smoother if he hadn't been all the dog he was.

But I'm getting ahead of my story. Let me begin at the beginning, before the first vapor materialized, before the league of phantasms assembled in my driveway, before the ghost bus, its air horn blasting, its shimmering, translucent passengers rattling rusty chains, came hurtling through my bedroom walls in the middle of the night.

But where does a story properly begin? When trouble

strikes and everything goes haywire? When the narrator turns a certain age? Or is it when the hero first enters the scene?

I don't know of any hard and fast rule.

Perhaps I should start with when I got my dog.

At first, to my disappointment, he wasn't my dog at all. He belonged to my next-door neighbor, Jip, a girl half a year older than I was, whose mother had decided that her daughter could use some cheering up. Since Jip was not only my neighbor but my friend, I tagged along when they went to pick out a puppy.

We drove for a long time. The sun was shining. The air was clear. A slight but steady breeze cooled the country-side. The morning's efforts at conversation had long since slipped into silence when a sign nailed to a fence post brought us to a momentary halt.

PUREBRED PUPPIES FOR SALE, it said.

Turning off the highway, we bounced and lurched along a rutted road. Rocks smacked into the floorboard like bullets fired from below by angry gophers. Twice I had to get out to open, then close, a wide wooden gate, and once, while I was struggling with an especially trou-blesome latch, a cow as big as a piano ambled over and pushed me with its broad, snotty nose, bringing a smile to Jip's wan face. Finally, after crossing a shallow stream, we came to a stone house surrounded by half a dozen tidy outbuildings and an untold number of barking dogs.

"Just imagine," Jip's mother observed. "All of this out here in the middle of nowhere."

The puppies—seven of them—were on the porch. No bigger than beanbag toys, they rolled and tumbled at our feet. Some were brown and white, some were black and white, some were entirely white except for their faces.

Jip was attracted to the smallest one, with smoother hair and shorter legs than his siblings, a full mask, and a constellation of black spots running from his shoulders to his rump.

"I'll take this one," she said.

The little dog accepted his fate without quarrel, licking Jip's fingers and crawling into her lap, where he curled up like a fat cheese tortellini and went to sleep. On the way home, Jip slept too, leaving me with little to do but think up names.

Lots of good ones came to mind, but because of the puppy's unique pattern of spots—black dots and dashes scattered along his paper white back like the random marks of a child's first drawing—by the time the car pulled into the driveway and my seatmates had opened their eyes, I could confidently announce that his name was Scribble.

At two pounds and two ounces, Scribble weighed less than a pot roast, and despite his fondness for naps, quickly revealed himself to be a temperamental terror, full of spit and vinegar, a high-speed, high-maintenance dogful of teeth—more than Jip and her mother had bargained for. Two weeks after she got him, and one day after a doctor sewed three stitches in her lower lip, Jip gave Scribble to me.

It's funny how something so small as a puppy can make such a big difference in your life. Scribble moved in on a Saturday. By Sunday, I had no doubt that he was the dog for me. His needs, like those of a human infant, were constant and many, but, in a happily compatible way, so were mine.

Of course, I had to make adjustments. The first one was waking up to take him outside. Normally, once my head comes into contact with a pillow, it stays there until the alarm clock sounds. But Scribble had other ideas. When the mood struck him, sometimes at sunrise, sometimes in the dark of night, he'd nuzzle my ear, tug my hair, nip my fingers, and snort and snuffle beneath the covers like a baby pig.

How could anybody sleep with that going on?

That's how I became accustomed to standing under the stars, listening to night creatures, newspaper trucks, passing trains, and the hum of the next-door neighbor's heat pump.

It's a different world after dark, more different than I ever imagined. But, of course, since I wasn't yet thirteen, I knew about only ordinary things, things that other people say they see—not that they're always right.

My name is Lawson, which isn't a common name, I admit, but even so, it's easy enough to spell, so you wouldn't think it'd be that hard to pronounce. But lots of people insist on calling me *Lar*son, or *Lor*son, and some even say *Glee*son, so that tells you something about people, docsn't it?

Humph!

There are so many excellent reasons to have a dog.

Mine is a Jack Russell terrier, a breed that's quite popular on TV, mainly because Jack Russell terriers are so smart that they can learn what to do faster than the actors can. Scribble is the smartest dog I've ever met, but because he's also the stubbornest, sometimes it's hard to tell. Take walks, for example. It's Scribble, not me, who decides where we'll go.

"C'mon, Scribble," I'll say. "Let's go this way."

But Scribble will tug in the opposite direction until I give up and follow him.

It may be that his willfulness is related to his sixth sense. I'm on somewhat shaky ground here, because the truth is, I don't know how many senses dogs are supposed to have. I know that some of their senses, like hearing and smell, are superior to those of humans, and given what dogs like to pick up and eat, I suspect that their sense of taste may be missing altogether. But beyond these, and touch, and ordinary eyesight, Scribble has a gift for perceiving the fourth dimension.

In other words, Scribble can see ghosts.

The first time it happened was on a morning walk, soon after Jip's mother put their house up for sale. Scribble had stopped to sniff at the pine needles that had accumulated under a tree near the pond.

Suddenly, he looked up and growled, clawing at the trunk, and lunging like a wild beast into the lower branches. I could see nothing, of course—not even a bird.

To anyone else, I suppose, the episode would have remained a mystery. But I'm not one to let things go unexplained.

For example, if I see a car speeding down the street, the first thing that occurs to me is that it's bank robbers on the lam. If I find a nickel, or a dime, or—lucky me—a quarter on the sidewalk, I figure that rich people must've passed this way doing handstands.

To my way of thinking, there's a logical explanation for everything.

So, after considering several hypotheses, I concluded that Scribble's agitation was caused by ghosts. My theory was that ghosts, sensitive to light, roost in trees during the heat of the day, not unlike mosquitoes that rise up from the water to nest in the cooling shade of leaves until the sun goes down.

Scribble, apparently, was born knowing this.

Perhaps if Jip's mother had been aware of Scribble's special ability, she wouldn't have been in such a hurry to get rid of him.

Like so many things in life, the facts don't become apparent until later on, and by then it's often much too late to do anything about it.

Believe me, I know.

As time went by, Scribble's outward appearance changed. His body grew longer faster than it became taller. For a while there, I worried that he might be turning into a dachshund—a German wiener dog—instead of a more properly proportioned terrier.

His white hair, which had started out soft and smooth like the downy fur of a cottontail rabbit, became coarse and unruly, partially obscuring the black markings that had inspired his name.

On his chin, whiskers appeared, like the face of an unshaven old man. His hairless parts—his tummy and the inside of his legs—previously a newborn baby pink, became dappled with brown, giraffelike spots.

Interestingly, these reminded me of Jip.

Jip's skin looked like confetti; she was freckled from head to toe.

I found those tiny tan shapes mesmerizing, like seashells, summer flowers, autumn leaves, or an abstract painting hanging in a museum. I could have studied Jip's patterns for hours, but she always made me stop. She said she hated the way she looked.

"But Jip," I'd say, "it's *you!*"

"That's the problem," she'd reply.

Scribble didn't help matters when he bit her the time that she knelt down to kiss him. After Jip's stitches came out, there was a thin jagged line on her lip. In my opinion, it was barely noticeable, but to Jip, after all she'd been through, it was the last straw.

Scribble's teeth were always getting him into trouble. Even when he was sitting quietly, he was chewing on something. Shoelaces. Shopping bags. Furniture legs. Rugs. The rubber bumper on the base of the vacuum cleaner. One day, he destroyed the remote control for the big-screen TV, a random act of vandalism that infuriated my mother.

The next day found me shopping for a replacement, plus a supply of rawhide bones. Only one store I know of carries both, and that's Wal-Mart, with nearly two hundred thousand square feet of everything you need and a great deal that you don't.

The bones came forty-eight to a package, in three flavors, natural, chicken, and Kansas City–style barbecue beef. Since the price was right, I got one of each. The remote control also was pretty reasonable, given that it claimed to work on TVs, VCRs, DVD players, stereos, and garage doors.

Had this been all there was to my shopping trip, it wouldn't be worth mentioning, but on my way to check out, I passed through the snack food aisle, and that's where I first saw him—a wiry, bent, bow-legged man in a blue baseball cap, a sort of senior-citizen Gumby, using his fingers to eat tuna fish from a can.

"Howdy," he said, sounding like the sidekick in an old Western movie. "Are y'all findin' everything y'all wanted?"

Y'all?

Puzzled, I turned around to see the people he was talking to. No one else was nearby.

"If you're addressing me," I replied, "I'm here by myself. I rode my bike from home."

"Int'resting," he said, eyeing the items in my cart. "I see y'all have a dog. Now, that's real good. I've always had a lot of respect for dogs. Even when they pee on your floor, they never make excuses."

Who is *this guy?* I wondered.

"Excuse me," I said, as politely as possible under the circumstances, "but I have to go."

"Sure thing, son," he replied, nodding. "Nice talking to y'all."

Now here's the amazing part: About ten minutes later, when I was opening one of the plastic bags of bones while Scribble jumped up and down, there on the cardboard flap at the top of the package was this guy's picture—and guess what? The person I'd been talking to was none other than Sam Walton, the founder of Wal-Mart. What was amazing was that Sam Walton not only was a legendary business genius, having started what eventually became the world's biggest company, but was also dead, and had been since 1992!

Holy smokes! I thought.

You could have knocked me over with a terrier!

Perhaps this is where my story ought to begin, with my first conversation with an emissary from the Other Side.

Or maybe I'm making this whole thing too hard.

Maybe it makes no difference where we start, or even what happens along the way. Maybe, when all is said and done, the only thing that matters is the ending.

But gosh, I hope not.

A Promise Made

Scribble was a small dog. At six months of age, he was almost as big as he was going to get, standing just twelve inches tall at the withers and weighing slightly over one pound per inch.

Despite his abbreviated stature, Scribble was fearless. Try as they might, the bigger dogs in the neighborhood didn't intimidate him, and only a top-quality retractable nylon band leash and my frantic shouts kept him from actually catching cars and trucks. So when I realized there were spirits afoot, I was glad to have Scribble at my side. I certainly didn't want to have to face them alone.

I also knew better than to tell anyone. People who claim to have seen ghosts sound crazy. They're so sure of themselves, for one thing, and they go on and on, for another, as if we were all interested in the details of their personal hallucinations.

Except, of course, for Jip. I could tell Jip anything—in complete confidence.

Jip was as smart as a whip. There was very little she didn't know *something* about. Except for the times when I was visiting her in her room, all she did was read. Among other subjects, Jip had become an authority on the paranormal: apparitions, ESP, out-of-body experiences, poltergeists, psychokinesis, reincarnation, automatic writing, preexistence—Jip had studied it all.

"The explained, Lawson, is only a fraction of the

unexplained," she said. "And the truth is a minuscule part of that."

"That's pretty small," I called from underneath her bed, where I was retrieving a peevish Scribble, interrupted while eating a spider.

"You bet it is," Jip replied. "Especially when it comes to the afterlife."

There was a long, uncomfortable silence, during which Jip fluffed her pillows and Scribble gave up the struggle, letting me hold him while he gnawed on my forearm.

"So how does it work?" I asked. "Do people come back as other people, or as animals, or as ghosts?"

"That's hard to say," Jip replied. "The evidence suggests it could be any one of those, or possibly even a flower or a rock. There's one thing you can count on, though—when I come back from being dead, you'll know it."

I didn't say anything.

It didn't seem right.

Here's what I think: People really need to learn to appreciate what's happening while it's happening, because time's up before you know it. In fact, it was only a few days after our last talk that time, like a tower built on sand, suddenly leaned over and collapsed, taking a good portion of my world with it. Entire days vanished without a trace. Weeks were shrouded in fog. The next thing I remember is Scribble trying to climb a pine tree while we walked by the pond.

"Down, boy," I commanded. "You'll hurt yourself."

Scribble responded with a growl, leaping into the air like a circus dog and snapping at pinecones on his way back down. Obviously, something in the tree had gotten his dander up, but when I looked through the prickly foliage, I saw nothing.

"C'mon now, Scribble," I said. "Relax."

It was quite cold, as I recall, a wintry Sunday morning—not the best of times to be out-of-doors trying to train a high-spirited dog. My fingers ached. My cheeks and chin were numb. All I wanted to do was go home.

Scribble, of course, had other ideas. Temporarily abandoning the trees, he had set his sights on the pond.

Since it hadn't rained for months, the pond was only two thirds full, with trash distributed in concentric rings like oddly shaped asteroids circling Saturn—pop bottles, plastic bags, sticks, balls, toys, mismatched shoes. And although the water was sealed over with ice, it gave off an aroma like a guinea pig cage—sour, rank, and foul.

Scribble, however, seemed to like it, which demonstrates one of the basic differences between humans and dogs. Jerking hard on the leash, he bounded to the water's edge, sniffed the earth, and barked at a half-submerged box. Then he flipped over and wriggled on the ground, smearing his back with natural salt, frozen mud, and concentrated pond stink. Thus armored, he turned around, dashed back to the pines, raised his head, and howled like a beagle.

"Dang, dog!" I cried. "What's the matter with you?"

Given his insistence that something was in the tree, I

decided to conduct a thorough, limb-by-limb search. That's when my understanding of the laws of the universe began to change.

With Scribble's leash in one hand, I reached out with both hands to part the thick, evergreen foliage and discovered to my astonishment that what I'd thought was a branch wasn't there. Even though I was looking right at it, when I attempted to push it aside, my hands slipped right through, as though the branch were only an illusion.

It had *some* substance, of course. It wasn't as if I were trying to touch a hologram—an image with no physical properties at all. But what there was had the filmy texture of cotton candy, and was sticky like cotton candy too. Bits of it clung to my fingers.

Right away, Scribble began to lick it off.

"Stop it, Scribble!" I cried. "You don't know what that stuff is!"

Here's something else I didn't know about ghosts: apparently, they can impart their characteristics to the things they touch, like a magnet rubbed on a needle. Stooping to scoop up Scribble, my hands passed through the little terrier's body as if he were a cumulus cloud.

"Holy smokes!" I shouted, letting go of Scribble's leash. "Now what?"

Did I really need to ask?

Scribble's peculiar condition was no different from my own. When he took off up the hill and ran through the fence surrounding the neighborhood swimming pool, I chased after him, passing through the upright bars as if I were an x-ray.

Huh? I thought.

Somehow, I had become neither solid, liquid, nor gas, but something in a wholly different state—a form of matter unknown in ordinary physics.

To Scribble, our situation was a game. Yapping happily, he dashed around the covered pool, daring me to catch him, pausing now and then to let me near, but always, at the last second, bounding out of reach.

Dang, but that's a fast dog! I thought.

Soon I was exhausted and had to give up the chase. Pleased with his victory, Scribble trotted through a concrete flower pot as if it were a shadow, flopping himself down by the edge of the pool.

Now, some dogs are like upholstered furniture. Where they sit is where they tend to stay. But Scribble was much too full of energy for that. If he'd had fingers, he would have drummed them on the sidewalk. If he'd been seated in a kitchen chair, he would have rocked it back and forth on two legs. As it was, he amused himself by gnawing at the rope suspending the heavy blue tarpaulin over the pool.

"Hey!" I called out. "Be careful!"

As Jip's ill-fated kissing experience had proved, a puppy's teeth are razor sharp. The nylon rope, crisscrossed and stretched like a giant shoelace, suddenly snapped apart, causing the tarp to slump with a sigh into the pool, nearly taking Scribble with it.

Startled, the little dog darted to the wrought-iron gate, where he abruptly stopped, turned around, and began barking at the pool cover, now sinking like a doomed ocean liner into the frigid water.

In a single, inspired moment, I made three scientific observations.

The first was that while open water, such as a pond, freezes when the surrounding air reaches a certain temperature, covered water, such as a swimming pool, does not.

The second was that if Scribble's teeth could cut rope, and the fence had brought him to a halt, then his ability to pass through solid objects—and likewise, mine—must have been only temporary.

And the third useful fact that leapt fully formed into my mind was that my dog and I were trapped!

The swimming pool, protected by an eight-foot-high iron barricade, is chained and padlocked in winter. Until ten o'clock on Memorial Day, no one is allowed inside. But that's where Scribble and I now found ourselves—caged, cold, and all alone, like a pair of polar bears after hours at the zoo.

Good grief! I thought.

I could climb it, I figured, although it wouldn't be easy. The metal bars were like ice. But what would I do with Scribble? He was too fragile to throw over the fence, too big to force through the openings, and if I tried to pull him up behind me with his leash, he'd strangle like a Wild West outlaw hanging from a noose.

Finally, to my intense discomfort, I stuffed my uncooperative companion inside my jacket and, balancing on a trash can, pulled myself to the top of the fence, where I teetered, slipped, and tumbled to the ground on the other side.

"*Ooof!*" I said.

Scribble was slow to forgive, sulking in our room for the rest of the day. Despite this unavoidable tiff, the episode proved worthwhile, providing me with invaluable information:

Ghost goo *was* like a magnet! Exactly like a magnetized needle, its effect faded quickly as the molecules of the exposed object returned to their natural state of disorder. Whatever powers these ghosts were inadvertently passing on were fleeting.

But while it lasts, I thought, *think of the possibilities!*

A Sight Unseen

Home is where the war is. At least, that was the situation at my house. Why Cornelia and Buzz had gotten married in the first place was as big a mystery to me as black holes in space, cosmic dust, and gravity waves.

With those two people, anything could provoke an argument—an unguarded expression, a careless thought, a poor choice of words . . . or simply a mutual sighting.

"Here's the newspaper," Buzz said, as Cornelia poured herself a cup of coffee.

16

"Don't tell me what to do!" Cornelia snapped. "I'm sick to death of you telling me what to do!"

"I don't care what you do," Buzz retorted. "All I said was 'Here's the paper.'"

"C'mon, Scribble," I whispered. "Let's go to our room."

For as long as I could remember, I'd had a room to myself, which I tried to keep, if not entirely clean, at least reasonably tidy. But when Scribble entered my life, housekeeping became a real challenge. All of a sudden, what had been *my* room was now *our* room. It was where Scribble slept at night, where he napped in the afternoon, and where he was confined when nobody else was home.

I kicked a ratty tennis ball into the corner and sat on the edge of the bed. Scribble jumped up beside me and rolled onto his back—his way of asking me to scratch his stomach.

When I complied, Scribble whimpered with pleasure.

I sneezed.

Dog hair.

All dogs shed, but some shed more than others. Wherever Scribble would alight, he'd leave tiny white hairs, each about the length and thickness of a human eyelash. I'd find them on my bed, my chair, my carpeting, and clinging to my clothes, and I suppose they were floating in the air that I breathed. A big plastic-cased electronic air purifier was supposed to solve that problem, but it wasn't entirely up to the task. What it did do, however, with its unwavering white noise, was mask the voices in the rest of the house, making my bedroom a very satisfactory retreat.

Here, I could think.

Sometimes I thought about my problems at school, sometimes about the trouble at home, but this time, even though I really didn't want to, what I thought about was my friend Jip.

I was finding it harder and harder to imagine her face—to conjure it up out of memory. I had no photographs of her of my own, and even the school yearbook was no help. Because she'd been sick, Jip had missed picture day.

Why couldn't I remember?

It seemed so strange.

I knew exactly what her nose looked like, and her eyes, her ears, her hair, her dimples, and her mouth, and, of course, all those freckles everywhere, but when in my mind I tried to put the parts together to form a face, I found that I couldn't.

Why?

I knew Jip as well as anybody. Better than that. I knew her as well as I knew myself. But though I could sense her while I sat in my room rubbing my dog—her dog—I couldn't see her, and I wanted to see Jip more than anything.

There's not a lot to be said for being invisible.

I lay on my back on the bed. Scribble licked my hand. Bright sunlight poured through the blinds, projecting a myriad of lines across the ceiling, wall-to-wall and all parallel, like the upright bars of a wrought-iron fence.

I wondered, *When Scribble and I passed through the swimming pool fence, what, exactly, happened to us?*

It seemed logical that our molecules had separated like particles of smoke, if *logic* is the right word for the process you use to make sense of the fourth dimension.

Next time, I told myself, *I'll try to pay attention.*

Once again I felt a sneeze coming on. When I raised my fingers to stifle it, tiny white hairs drifted down like snowflakes, and the hand that I'd been scratching Scribble's stomach with smelled vaguely like a ferret.

Scribble was due for a bath.

There's only one way to bathe a high-energy dog, and that's to get into the shower with him. While Scribble stood in the warm spray, I showered, then sat down in the bottom of the tub and soaped him from head to toe, a procedure that he not only tolerated but seemed to enjoy—probably because it involved a massage.

Scribble's markings change in the shower. The force of the water parts his scruffy white outer coat, and his black spots, partially hidden like icebergs in a whitecapped sea, become bigger, more numerous, more defined.

As I rinsed him with the spray arm, the stray marks on his back intensified until I could make out a shape—a face, if I used my imagination, like people do when they say they see a man in the moon. But with no nose, oblong eyes, and a wide, turned-up mouth, it was only the barest representation of a face, a caricature neither lunar nor human, like the smiley face found on bumper stickers, socks, underwear, and ties, and featured in a number of silly singing television commercials for Wal-Mart.

In her last letters to me, Jip had used a tiny smiley face to dot the letter *i*.

Fortunately for Scribble, the image disappeared beneath his guard hairs when I toweled him off.

The next day, Scribble chewed the buttons off the remote control, and the day after that I had my first conversation with Sam Walton's ghost.

Then my life got weird.

For one thing, it snowed, the first measurable precipitation the region had experienced in seventy-one days. And while it was hardly what you'd call a blizzard—only five dry, fluffy, frozen inches—because it fell late at night before the snowplows had time to clear the streets, it was just enough to close the schools.

What luck! And Scribble loved it!

He dug his nose in the snow, peed on it, and ran back and forth, forming a crisscrossed network of Scribble tracks. When the sun broke through the high, gray clouds and the colors of the landscape switched from sepia and white to Kodachrome, Scribble decided we should take a walk.

There are two reasons to walk your dog. One is to aid his digestion, which is why responsible dog owners always carry plastic shopping bags. The other is to give your dog an interesting life.

This latter reason was my objective for Scribble.

With classes suspended, my parents quarreling, and Jip no longer living next door, I saw no reason to deny my pet and partner this special canine pleasure. I let him lead us on a long, long walk, past the pond, past the school, past the shopping center, all the way to the cemetery out by the expressway.

Except for the constant, mind-numbing rumble of cars and trucks going by, Pleasant Ridge was a peaceful place. Scribble and I were its only visitors. With just a few gravesites remaining since the new ramp had been built, most people preferred to be buried someplace else.

I'd been here once before, at a time when I was hardly in the mood for sightseeing. Scribble had never been here at all. Nevertheless, he immediately began conducting a grave-to-grave search, pawing at the snow, snorting like a pony, sniffing at every object he came across, his stubby half tail held high. From headstone to headstone we hurried, pausing at each icy slab of granite for a second or two, like vacationers in an art museum whose tour bus is about to leave.

Working our way along the perfectly aligned rows, I was fascinated by the many ways people decorated the final resting places of their loved ones. I would have expected vases filled with plastic flowers, and, to be sure, there were plenty of those, representing most of the common cultivated species of plants and flowers, but to my everlasting enlightenment there were also family photos,

21

trinkets, personal artifacts, sacred objects, decorative gim-cracks, and children's toys.

At one impressive plot, wind chimes topped with danc-ing cherubs dangled from a six-foot shepherd's crook. At another, a bronze butterfly as big as my head swayed back and forth in the breeze. Carved rocks, framed drawings, bundled feathers, ceramic statuettes, dolls, balls, booties, wood carvings, and seashell art peeked up through the snow, each apparently a loving remembrance of things past.

Occasionally, the living sought to entertain the dead with spinning pinwheels, tiki torches, flags, banners, and Mylar balloons reading HAPPY BIRTHDAY, HAPPY ANNIVER-SARY, and, curiously, CONGRATULATIONS. Viewed as a whole, Pleasant Ridge took on the eerie ambiance of an abandoned bazaar.

Beside a polished stone bench topped with a mound of new-fallen snow, Scribble found what he'd come for. It was the plainest of markers, just a small block of gray stone stuck upright in the ground. On the front, in letters less than two inches high, a name had recently been carved.

JENNIFER IRIS PALMER.

Initials J-I-P.

Jip.

Silently, the dog dropped onto the snow, lay his head on his forelegs, and closed his eyes.

How did he know? I wondered. *How did he know?*

Phantom Light

I spent a lot of time at Jip's house. And why not? She was nice-looking, easy-going, well read, and sympathetic to my plight. Not only that, but only a narrow patch of trampled grass and a concrete driveway separated her house from mine.

Proximity is destiny.

Do that which lies closest to thy hand.

But Jip was no ordinary girl next door. Attractive, self-assured, intellectually superior, she had her quirky side, that's for sure. At one point, several weeks before Scribble came on the scene, Jip became convinced that ghosts were hiding in her house.

It wasn't a traditional sort of haunting, she explained, like the haunted houses that you hear about at Halloween. These were concentrated, densely packed essences who'd taken up refuge in bottles, jars, and appliances.

"I can't stand it, Lawson," she confessed. "They come spewing out like pressurized gas. Honestly, I'm afraid to squeeze the toothpaste for fear of what'll come out of the tube."

"You've actually seen them?" I asked.

"*See* is one of those words that covers a lot of ground," Jip replied. "Let me put it this way: There's absolutely no doubt in my mind that they were there."

"Hmmm," I said. "I'm beginning to understand."

"Don't patronize me, Lawson," Jip warned. "I

wouldn't make up something like this. Besides, I can prove it. Hand me that envelope."

Jip pointed to a bright yellow packet on top of her dresser.

"This one?" I asked.

"That's it," she confirmed. Jip slipped a handful of glossy snapshots from the envelope. "Here," she said, offering them to me. "Take a look at these."

The photograph on top was entirely blank, with not a shape, not a blur, not a speck on it. The next one was exactly like the first, as was the one after that, and the one after that. In fact, every single picture in the stack was as empty as the space between the stars.

"Did you order double prints?" I asked. "Or perhaps twenty-three reprints?"

"No way," Jip replied. "It's just a regular roll."

"It looks like your film got exposed to light," I observed.

"Exactly!" Jip confirmed. "Now do you believe me?"

"Excuse me?" I said, flipping through the photos a second time. "Unless you were trying to take pictures of the sun, all you have here is evidence of some kind of mistake."

"Lawson, Lawson, Lawson," Jip responded. "Don't you get it? It wasn't human error that spoiled those pictures. It was supernatural meddling. It's obvious that my film was blasted into blankness by phantom light."

"Phantom light?" I repeated.

"A self-contained, low-level energy source radiating from the fourth dimension," Jip explained. "Or, to put it in layman's terms, there was a ghost inside the camera."

I took a deep breath. Jip, I reminded myself, had not been feeling her best for quite some time.

"In that case," I replied, returning the photographs to the top of the bureau, "you probably should have your camera cleaned."

Now, of course, I'm ashamed to have been so openly skeptical. Not only was Jip six months older; she was far ahead of me in many other ways, as well. She knew then what I've only recently come to understand: nothing is more peculiar than the truth.

Indeed, as anyone more than twelve years of age has surely discovered, the bigger the secret, the weirder it seems. When I look at Cornelia and Buzz, for example, I just shake my head.

I've said it before, but there's no harm in saying it again: thank goodness for Scribble. Sometimes I think he bit Jip just so he could save me from a lifetime of ignorance.

But dogs, like knowledge, don't come cheap. Even a free one costs a bundle—easily a thousand dollars or more in the very first year. Most of the money goes for food, equipment, supplies, and routine medical attention, including shots and neutering, and you'll spend even more if you decide to put in a fence.

Scribble didn't have a fenced yard. When he wanted

to go out, I had to take him. This was how it happened that, one particular night, I was outside in my pajamas with the temperature hovering near zero on the Fahrenheit scale.

The stars seemed much closer to the earth than they appear on TV, but the moon, in celestial shadow, had melted to an icy sliver. The usual sounds—distant cars, passing cats, rustling leaves, the heat pump on the house next door—were strangely absent. Only my breathing, and Scribble's porcine snuffling, threatened the unnatural tranquillity.

Suddenly, in mid-whiz, Scribble froze. With a snarl, he raised his tail, tucked his right leg, tilted his head, and pointed like a well-trained bird dog. Just as you'd find the Big Dipper's pointer stars to locate the North Star, my eyes followed my little terrier's nose to the driveway, where to my astonishment a crowd of semitransparent, phosphorescent beings were floating shoulder to shoulder, just above the ground, approximately twelve across and more than twenty deep.

One of these spirits, wearing a baseball cap and hovering a few feet in front of the others, waved to me. I'm not exactly sure, but I think it might have been Sam Walton. Unfortunately, the episode was over in a matter of seconds—plus the light was in my eyes.

While individually none of the spooky specters gave off more illumination than your average table lamp, the glow from the fully assembled group was considerable, flickering and pulsating as if electrically charged—a kind of mini–aurora borealis—bright enough to do homework by.

Oh, how I wished that Jip were there with me. This was a supernatural spectacle right up her alley.

Of course, so many thoughts go through one's mind at a time like this: *Am I dreaming? Have I died? Why didn't I buy an inexpensive, single-use camera?* And finally, the one that really matters: *What do they want with me?*

But that's the trouble with such sightings. By the time you collect your thoughts enough to ask ghosts why they've come, they're gone.

It must be like skiing off a mountain, getting shot, or being hit by a car, because the survivors of such episodes always report, "Everything happened so fast." That was precisely my experience with these driveway phantasms. Zip! Flash! Poof!

If I ever get around to writing my life story, I'm going to call it *Suddenly.*

Jip once told me that if she wrote a memoir, she'd title it *Not Long for This World,* but then she confessed that she'd never actually sit down to do it because the writing process is much too time-consuming. Jip was very conscious of how she spent her time.

"Do you realize, Lawson," she told me, "that most people's lives are essentially wasted? When they're not performing some sort of predetermined, scripted act— basically just pretending—they're sitting in the audience watching other people perform."

"Well," I replied, "except for school."

"*Especially* school," Jip countered. "Trust me."

I couldn't be sure if Jip meant what she said. Sometimes, I suspected, she was putting on an act for me. Her brave front in the face of adversity, for one thing. And a lot of her observations, criticisms, commentary, and advice, for another.

Once, to avoid what was going on at home, I stayed at Jip's house after dark. We'd been talking about how you can't change other people, no matter how hard you try, when Jip piped up with a suggestion.

"When you go home tonight, Lawson, while your parents are sleeping," she said, "I want you to paint a double yellow line through the middle of each room, like the lines down the center of highways that mean 'Do Not Pass.' Then, when your parents wake up, everything will be clearly separated, with half the house set aside for one of them, and half for the other. It's the perfect solution. They'll never have to deal with each other again."

I thought about Jip's concept of divided rooms at her funeral, where rows of scarred, wooden pews were bisected by a single center aisle. School officials, teachers, and former classmates and their parents sat on one side. Jip's relatives clustered together on the other. It was a completely arbitrary barrier, consisting of nothing but a few feet of highly polished vinyl tile, but no one, to my recollection, dared to cross it.

This must be how things work with the Other Side, I figured. Contact between this world and the fourth dimension is limited, not because there's no way to get

through, but because both sides prefer to keep to themselves.

Unless there's a really compelling reason to cross over.

Something must be causing these sightings, I realized.
Something quite extraordinary.

Why else would leagues of phantoms leave magic goo
in evergreens and light up my driveway like Christmas?

Shopping for Answers

Dogs are not allowed in Wal-Mart. I'm not sure why that
is. Maybe it's because the store is already too crowded—
not with people, necessarily, but with stuff. Displays and
kiosks flank the main entrance. Piles of merchandise block
the aisles. Signs dangle from the ceiling, perch on top of
products, and stick out from the shelves. As big as Wal-
Mart is, you get the feeling that there's barely enough
room for the customers.

Reluctantly, I'd left Scribble dozing on the couch. I
could have used his special abilities on this trip, for I was
in Wal-Mart not to purchase household supplies but to
shop for answers. If the spirits were suddenly beginning to
show themselves, I figured that the migrating ghost of Sam
Walton could probably tell me why.

Of course, with maybe three thousand Wal-Marts
located all over the world, if the late founder were
still involved in his business, it was unlikely that I'd find

him twice in the same store—not to mention the one right up the street from me. But long odds are no reason to refuse to make an effort.

In the tuna fish section, I saw only a stout, orange-haired woman with a cartful of sixty-four-ounce jars of artificial marshmallow creme. No one was in school and office supplies. Polyester sheets, pillowcases, and shams was clear. Ditto for the plastic lampshade aisle. But at men's bagged socks and underwear, a huddle of comparison shoppers blocked the aisle, forcing me to go around the long way, past a table piled high with closeout DVDs.

How can they afford to sell products at prices like these? I wondered.

After examining every title, none of which I'd actually ever heard of, I chose one to take home.

Cruising through fabric paint, sequins, and beads; car batteries and novelty floor mats; pellet guns, paintball sets, and crossbows; and battery-powered, motorized toddler toys; I hit another human logjam at a display of painted flower pots, where the acrid aroma of lawn fertilizer with weed control made my eyes water and my nose run.

Just past the aisle of diet supplements, I spotted an old man sniffing a scented bar of bath soap. His back was turned, so I slowed down long enough to determine that he was shorter than the person I was searching for. After doubling back and retracing my steps through ninety-nine -cent greeting cards, vacuum cleaners, tropical fish, and bulk potholder loops, I finally had to face facts: the late Sam Walton was not to be found at Wal-Mart.

It's no good going looking for ghosts, I thought. *You have to let them come to you.*

To my annoyance, long lines had formed at the checkout. Even the twelve-items-or-less lane was stacked six deep. Kids cried for candy while their mothers read tabloid magazines for free. One woman was balancing her checkbook. Another was staring off into space, humming church music.

In front of me, a man looked at his watch and muttered, "What could be taking them so long? Don't they know I'm in a hurry?"

The process did seem to be slower than usual. Perhaps, I speculated, the computers were down or the manager was breaking in a trainee.

Oh, well, I thought. *I've gotten this far, I might as well see it through.*

But as the line crept forward, I began to question why I'd bothered to stay in it. It wasn't as if I needed the item in my hand, an old black-and-white movie called *Topper Returns,* about a woman ghost who persuades her next-door neighbor to catch the guy who killed her. It was just that it was irresistibly cheap.

Finally, after what seemed like forever, I was almost next in line. That's when I saw—or overheard, actually— what the holdup was.

Nothing was wrong with the cash registers, and no one was training the clerk, who seemed to understand perfectly well how to scan stuff and slide it into Wal-Mart's filmy blue plastic bags. The problem was with what else he was doing, namely, talking to every customer in line, yammering and yakking without letup, as if he had all the time in the world.

"Hey, how y'all doin'? What's the baby's name?" I heard him say. "Did y'all find everything okay? I've got a pain in my side, let me tell y'all. Had it since I got up this morning. How 'bout that president of ours? Isn't he somethin'? And so's his wife, now that I think about it."

One glance at the jabbering clerk was all it took.

You know how you look when you take your hat off? How your hair gets smushed down on top of your head? Well, this guy had hat hair to beat the band, as if he'd gone to bed with his hat on and didn't remove it until he got to work. Dressed in a light blue smock decorated with stickers, slogan buttons, and over thirty years' worth of service pins, the gnarled old blabbermouth was sporting a nametag that identified him as Johnson. But he wasn't fooling me—not for a minute. This guy was a dead ringer for Sam Walton.

"Hello, sonny boy," he greeted me when it was my turn. "Y'all got yourself a movie? It's too nice a day to be inside watching movies. Now, me, if I didn't have to work, I'd be out hunting. Ever been hunting?"

"Not for animals," I answered. "But I *was* hunting for a person—or something that looks a lot like one. Do you mind if I ask you a few questions?"

"Fire away," the Sam Walton look-alike replied. "I'm in no particular hurry. Not anymore."

In line behind me, a woman let out a loud groan.

"Do you remember me?" I asked him. "I was in here last week."

"Hmmm," he replied. "What's your name?"

"Lawson," I said. "With a *w* in the middle."

"Nice to see y'all," he responded, extending a liver-spotted hand across the counter. "Call me Johnson."

"All right," I agreed, giving him a conspiratorial wink. "If you're more comfortable with that."

"Oh, for heaven's sake!" the woman behind me grumbled. "Ask your question, why don't you!"

"Sorry," I told her. "This'll just take a minute." Turning to "Johnson," I inquired, "What's it like being on the Other Side?"

"Well," he replied, scratching his chin with his thumb and forefinger, "it's good and it's bad. The good thing is you get to meet a lot of nice people. The bad thing is that after a while, your feet hurt."

"I see," I responded.

"This is intolerable," the woman behind me complained. "All I came in for was a pot scrubber."

"Just one more question, and he's all yours," I promised her, before returning to the garrulous clerk. "Mr. Johnson," I said, "I've been seeing some strange things lately, things that are hard to explain, so I was wondering: Is there something you want to tell me?"

"Why, as a matter of fact, there is," he replied.

"I thought so," I said, relieved. "Okay, shoot."

"Y'all's total comes to four-twenty-four," he

announced. "And, hey, don't forget to have a nice day."

"Well," expelled the woman behind me, "finally!"

In the Dark

More than three hundred years ago in Japan, it was against the law to ignore a dog. The punishment was as severe as it gets: found guilty, and you could be put to death. Nowadays, however, should you overlook the needs of man's best friend, you're simply expected to be ashamed of yourself.

I took no chances. When Scribble tunneled up through the covers and licked my face, I pulled myself out of bed, put on my slippers and a fleece-lined jacket, and took him outside.

Once you've abandoned the idea of sleep, being up in the middle of the night can be very pleasant. In the glow of the streetlights, frost crystals forming on the lawn mirrors the twinkling of the stars. The night music of passing trains, distant sirens, and unseen, migrating geese has a haunting quality, which, if not revealed to be the sounds of displaced spirits, is comforting in a strange, primitive sort of way.

The best part is that when you're outside in the dark with your dog on a leash and your bed is just a few steps away, it's easy to imagine that you live alone. No one is fighting. No one's complaining. No one is telling you what to do. It's just you, your dog, and the darkness in a world rich with possibility.

Scribble stretched himself as terriers do, first the front end, then the back, followed by a full, gaping yawn. Revived, he trotted to a skinny, leafless sapling between the sidewalk and the curb, one of a whole streetful of plantings held in place with wires and wooden stakes.

That such trees survive is testimony to nature's tenacity. Typically non-native species chosen for the symmetrical shape and abundant spring blossoms, these displaced decorative accessories are stuck into shallow holes, watered once, and abandoned, where ever after they're a message post for passing dogs.

Why can't people be as tough as trees? I wondered.

If I'd have asked Jip that question, she would have answered that we're all the same—people, trees, dogs, grass, stars—everything—we're all made from the same raw material, which some say is atoms, some say is quarks, and some, more recently, have decided is energy strings, but according to Jip, all of it may be simply our imagination.

"We could be dreaming, Lawson," she speculated. "In which case, there's little to be gained by complaining. When we wake up, everything will be different."

For Jip's sake, I hope she's right.

Scribble, tired of standing in the front yard, tugged against his leash.

"Not now, Scribble," I told him. "We have to go back to bed."

But Scribble, as I frequently point out, had other plans. He strained against his collar until it began to choke him.

"All right," I relented. "But just for a few minutes."

Lest I change my mind, Scribble broke into a run all the way to the bottom of the hill, but as soon as we turned the corner and headed up the next street, he settled into his regular routine of sniffing, digging, and peeing.

A fog was coming in, forming halos around the streetlights. Inside the houses, on block after block, all was dark. The world, or one side of it, at least, was asleep. But when I followed Scribble into a cul-de-sac, where half a dozen same-size houses faced one another in forced familiarity, like villagers gathered at a well, a flickering blue light in an upstairs bedroom indicated that a television was on.

Was someone unable to sleep? Or had the person inside nodded off while watching TV? Perhaps there'd been an urgent phone call and he'd turned on the television to calm his nerves. With me out here and him—or was it her?—in there, I couldn't know, of course. I could only make up stories.

Is this what it's like on the Other Side? I wondered.

Night-walking offers hints of the world to come, a world in which we sense those we've left behind, but at a distance, separated by walls and time and darkness.

Under these conditions, communication is difficult.

Communication.

What if? I wondered.

Despite the brushoff my question had elicited from

"Johnson," there had to be a reason that I'd been experiencing all these sightings: ghost residue in trees, a crowd of phantoms in my driveway, the return of the charismatic founder of Wal-Mart.

What if Jip is trying to get in touch with me? I wondered.

Not all that long ago, eavesdropping on spirits was considered to be normal behavior. Séances, in which people held hands, closed their eyes, and exchanged a few words with dead friends and relatives, were almost as popular as the movies. And no self-respecting home was without a Ouija board, a tabletop alphabet with see-through pointer that with a nudge from willing hands spelled out cryptic messages from beyond the tomb, one spooky letter at a time.

Haunted houses, busy graveyards, the living possessed by the dead—such things once were the stuff of everyday life. But nowadays, everyone's a skeptic. Science tells us that whatever can't be repeated in a controlled experiment doesn't exist.

Hogwash! I say. Baloney!

Not everything in the universe submits to our will.

Some things will always be mysteries.

Take automatic writing, for example. As in a séance, a spirit-sensitive person called a medium goes into a trance, but instead of speaking in the voice of a departed loved one, the medium takes dictation, writing down words on a piece of paper faster than most people can think.

Jip was especially enthusiastic about this method.

"Not only do you hear from those who've gone ahead," she explained, "but you get a hard copy of what they had to say. It's like receiving a fax from the Other Side."

If Jip were trying to get in touch with me, I reasoned, no doubt she'd try her hand at automatic writing. But, knowing her, she wouldn't put all her eggs in one mailbox, so to speak. She'd also attempt other ways to get through, sending go-betweens such as Sam Walton or recruiting clubs of the recently deceased, and perhaps even entering and controlling my dreams.

Jip was a very resourceful person.

Jip, I thought with a sudden ache, *are you out there?*

As if in reply, wind chimes tinkled from a nearby deck. Scribble, who'd paused to leave his calling card on a clump of ornamental grasses, raised his head.

Suddenly, from out of the darkness, something brushed my ear, something filmy flying past my face. Scribble let out a single sharp bark. As for me, I was too startled to scream.

When my wits came back to me, I turned around. Flapping harmlessly from the branches of a curb tree was a plastic Wal-Mart bag, apparently ensnared while traveling on the breeze.

I'd been spooked by runaway trash.

"Settle down, Scribble," I instructed. "It's okay."

Almost as surprising as the low-flying litter was the abrupt arrival of day. In the dim light of night, our eyes dilate, opening ever wider to make out objects in our path. Dawn creeps in much in the same way, gradually electrifying the sky with a firefly glow, until all of a sudden morning breaks, bringing yesterday's troubles with it.

Yesterday's troubles.

That's the thing about missing somebody who's not coming back. It's almost impossible to move on. It's like trying to live without food. No matter what you do to keep yourself from thinking about it, the hunger never goes away. The days never get any better.

The Writer

Although I had no experience with automatic writing, it seemed to me that if one is going to attempt such a thing, one should use a good pen.

In my family's house, we kept a drawer full of writing instruments whose common characteristic was that they didn't work very well: dull, stubby, chewed-up pencils without erasers; dried-out felt-tip markers; highlighters with smashed points; ballpoint pens from banks, dentists, insurance companies, motels, and copy centers that skipped across the paper or ran out of ink in the middle of the page.

I once asked why we kept so many of them if they were so unreliable, and my mother answered that it was because of their poor quality that we needed them all.

"It's about the only thing around here that you can

count on," she explained. "When one fails to do the job, you simply get another."

Later on, I was to realize that this was my mother's approach to many things in life, but at that moment my rejection of her philosophy was limited to the task at hand. Inferior writing equipment may be okay for grocery lists, I concluded, but when it came to transcribing a message from Jip, I didn't want to take any chances.

I needed a new pen.

During the uneventful bike ride to Wal-Mart, it occurred to me that it would be possible to find yourself inside that store every single day of the year. Face it: there's always something that you need. Yet, curiously, even though the store claims to save you money, when I received my change, I discovered I was almost broke.

Hmmm, I thought. *Maybe I shouldn't have gotten the ten–theme book Valu-Pak or the party bucket of malted milk balls.*

The pen, however, was an excellent choice. It had a walnut base, a brushed-chrome cap, and, welded to the clip, a tiny, three-dimensional statuette of a world-famous cartoon rabbit. Unlike a skinny, lightweight, disposable pen, this practical collectible was reassuringly round, with a serious heft to it. A pen like this gave the feeling that the words that would come forth from it would definitely be words worth keeping.

When performing automatic writing, the instrument is only one factor to consider. Where to seat yourself may be equally important. As with a satellite dish, a portable radio, or playground-quality walkie-talkies, reception was likely to vary according to the position of the receiver.

Would a sunny spot be better, I wondered, or should I try to write in the dark? Indoors or outside? Upstairs or downstairs? Standing, sitting, squatting, or lying down?

There was no way to know for sure.

But privacy had to matter, I figured, and so did comfort. I wouldn't want to be interrupted in the middle of an important transmission, and if it was an especially long one, I wouldn't want to risk my hand getting tired.

I concluded that the best place to be for performing automatic writing was the best place to be, period: in my bed, propped up on pillows, pen poised for action, the blinds closed, the lights out, my faithful dog resting at my feet.

Unfortunately, when I peeled off the plastic wrap from the bulk pack of notebooks, Scribble pounced on it before it hit the floor.

"Drop it!" I commanded.

Ignoring me, Scribble shook the crinkly plastic back and forth, as if trying to break its neck, then sat down and began to chew it into a soppy wad. For his safety, and at some risk to mine, I tugged the wrapper from his teeth.

"Give me a break, Scribble," I complained. "I'm trying to do something important here."

With a whimper, he jumped into the bed and lay his chin across my foot. "That's better," I told him.

Twisting the cap of my new pen half a turn to the right, I opened a green-covered theme book, leaned against

41

my pillows, and waited to be inspired.

There are seventy sheets of paper in a basic wire-spiral theme book—one hundred and forty pages, if you count both sides. Each wide-ruled sheet has space for twenty-six lines. Each line holds an average of seven words, written in cursive with a wide-tip pen. That's one hundred and eighty-two words per page, for a total of more than twenty-five thousand words when you fill up the book. I know this because I figured it out while writing my name, waiting for a message from Jip.

As Scribble snoozed, either from obedience or boredom, I wrote "Lawson" over and over again, starting each one with a great swooping *L* in a fine forward slant and concluding with a mere squiggle of an *n*. Sixteen hundred times I repeated this, until I'd covered nearly nine pages with script.

Well, this is a bust, I thought.

I sat up, straightened my shoulders, popped my neck, and shook the cramp from my wrist. Scribble stirred slightly but continued to snooze.

Maybe I'm doing it wrong, I thought.

I flipped back through my work. Every page looked the same: "Lawson, Lawson, Lawson," one after another, running on and on and on. The repetition was so exact it could have passed for wallpaper—pretty disappointing for nearly two hours' worth of work.

But on a second, more careful review, something caught my eye: on the sixth page, two lines from the bottom, near the right margin, jamming the line's last "Lawson" against a prepunched hole, I spied the single, short, out-of-place word, "Hey."

Blinking, I looked again. There was no mistake. It was a capital *H*, a small *e*, and a long, looping, lowercase *y*. Now that I'd seen it, it stuck out like a big black spot on the back of a small white dog.

"Lawson, Lawson, Lawson, Lawson, Lawson, Hey, Lawson," the line read.

Huh? I thought. *"Hey, Lawson"?*

I don't remember writing this!

Was someone trying to get my attention?

Was a spirit—Jip, perhaps—engaged in tapping me on the shoulder, so to speak?

Quickly, while the spell was still on me, I settled back into the pillows and started a brand-new page.

"Lawson, Lawson, Lawson," I began, as Scribble crawled beneath the bedspread to resume his nap.

As before, the "Lawsons" flowed without letup, but because by now my hand was cramping, they came more slowly, with bigger, sloppier characters and fewer names per page. Also, because my eyes were closed to help induce a trance, the letters no longer stayed within the lines.

After half a dozen more pages of this, the ache in my right wrist had become a severe, throbbing pain. Just when I was sure that I couldn't go on any longer, I sensed that something about my output had changed—an unplanned wobble, an inadvertent squiggle, a sudden dot—something that when you put it all together did not spell "Lawson."

The ghost writer had returned!

"Now we're talking!" I said out loud, opening my eyes to read along.

How many times have I wished I'd kept them shut?

Too many to recall.

My outburst, although not all that loud, contrasted sufficiently with the silent room that it awakened Scribble, his sleepy head emerging from the covers just inches from my weary hand. The sight of the cartoon-rabbit writing instrument wiggling erratically across the paper like a wounded varmint triggered the dog's deepest, most primitive instincts.

With the suddenness of a spring-loaded trap, he clamped his teeth around the pen, snatched it from my grasp, and took off running down the hall.

"SCRIBBLE!" I screamed. "Come back here!"

I might as well have been trying to command the wind. Scribble recognized no authority. The fragile connection with the spirit world, established at such personal sacrifice, was now irretrievably lost.

I finally found my pen under the sofa cushions. Except for scratches on the base and a slight depression in the cap, it had held up to Scribble's jaws remarkably well. There's a lot to be said for quality.

An examination of my theme book yielded a happy surprise. At the conclusion of all those big, loopy

"Lawsons" were the words "What's happening?" complete with apostrophe and question mark.

There could be no doubt about it now. Just as she'd promised, the persistent Jip had managed to get a message through.

"Hey, Lawson," she'd transmitted. "What's happening?"

Chit-Chat

It's been said that one reason dogs are man's best friend is that dogs can't talk. By this, I suppose people mean that dogs can't disagree with you, or interrupt you, or bore you with opinions on politics or details of their dreams. But to my way of thinking, whoever came up with this explanation couldn't be more wrong. Conversation is the best part of friendship. Nothing can take the place of being with someone you really care about and sharing your innermost thoughts.

I guess that's why I missed Jip so much.

"When I grow up," she once told me, "I'd like to be one of those people out in Los Angeles or New York who decides what programs to put on TV. I'd make a lot of changes. But I'd also like to be a physicist, supervising research into the nature of matter, eventually perfecting the Theory of Everything. And for a while, I want to serve in the United States Congress as the chairman of the House Appropriations Committee."

"I don't know what I want to be," I said. "I just hope that whatever it is, it doesn't require getting up too early. I think I may be sleep deprived."

"I guess that rules out school crossing guard," Jip observed. "Too bad, too. You would have been so good at it."

"Do you think you'll ever get married?" I asked her.

"Sure I will," Jip immediately replied. "Several times. How about you?"

"I doubt it," I confessed. "It seems like it's an awful lot of trouble."

"Life is what you make of it, Lawson," Jip philosophized. "Except, of course, for the parts you can't do anything about."

Such heartfelt chit-chat would go on for hours. Jip and I talked about music, art, religion, history, and the origin of life on earth. She showed me how to cheat at cards, wiggle my ears, fold homework into paper flowers, and bounce spitballs off the spinning blades of her ceiling fan. She gave me advice on dealing with the teachers at school, strangers on the phone, and anybody who asks for money, and when we played the word game Boggle, she invariably won. When the conversation waned, Jip sang old love songs a cappella.

She was truly one of a kind.

And now, with, "Hey, Lawson, what's happening?" staring at me from my theme book, I found that I could think of nothing else. That these four words could be interpreted by others as the most trivial of greetings made absolutely no difference to me. Knowing who it was from, I treasured the brief, dictated phrase as if it were a handmade Valentine, carefully detaching the pages from the spiral wire and hiding them under my pillow—a risky proposition given Scribble's predisposition to ferret out unfamiliar objects and chew them to shreds.

Her words had not come easy. Out of nearly two thousand and two hundred separate words that I'd written down, only four seemed to be from Jip—three if I excluded "Lawson." That's a success rate little better than panning for gold in the neighborhood flood-control pond.

Obviously, I needed to improve my technique.

But how?

My eyes fell on *Topper Returns*, the ghost story/murder mystery/romantic comedy DVD that I'd bought on impulse at Wal-Mart. According to the notes on the back, it was released in 1941.

Holy smokes! I thought. *That's more than sixty years ago!*

But what's time to people on the Other Side?

Maybe I'd pick up some pointers.

With a steaming bag of popcorn fresh from the microwave oven, I flopped onto the sofa and clicked on the DVD player. Old-fashioned, handwritten titles flew to the foreground to fill the screen.

It takes a while for the story of *Topper Returns* to get under way. First, there's a gunshot that misses its mark, then a near miss from a falling chandelier, and finally, a clumsy midnight stabbing that succeeds but turns out to be a fatal case of mistaken identity.

Throughout this setup, Scribble, bored and restless, made a thorough pest of himself, shoving his nose into my popcorn, chewing the cushions, biting my arm, and whining incessantly to go outside.

It can't be true what they say about dogs' seeing only in black and white, because Scribble showed not the slightest bit of interest in the flickering, monochromatic images on the television screen. Eventually he gave up and went to sleep.

The ghost sequences in *Topper Returns* have both their pluses and their minuses. There are blowing curtains, floating household objects, magically appearing footprints, and doors and windows that open and shut by themselves. Sometimes the ghost woman looks like a regular person, sometimes she's invisible, and occasionally, you can see through her as if she were a frosted windowpane. In one scene this surprisingly lively murder victim bends down and zips herself into invisibility, feet first.

I found it surprising that she could materialize at will. I would have figured that crossing over to the Other Side was a lot harder than that. But what really got my attention happens near the end. While trying to get away, the guy who committed the murder is killed in a car crash. Now a ghost himself, when confronted by his victim, he readily admits his guilt, and at her insistence writes his confession down on the back of an envelope, which subsequently is passed around to everybody in the cast, including the formerly clueless cops.

Mystery solved.

Case closed.

As Scribble slept with his head on my arm, I concluded that the message of the movie is this: Although ghosts may not be easy to see, their handwritten messages are.

Perhaps I'm struggling unnecessarily, I thought. *Jip may be capable of writing things down for herself.*

Night School

They say childhood is the best of times, but they must have forgotten how much of it is spent taking orders from grownups. Whenever adults don't understand what's demanding your attention, they always feel obliged to come up with something else for you to do.

Ironically, by spending so much time hidden behind closed doors, I'd made myself conspicuous. Add to this Scribble's increasingly unpopular stubborn streak, and I suppose it was inevitable that the two of us would wind up attending night school.

"You need structure in your life," my mother announced. "And that nasty little dog of yours needs to learn some manners."

To my surprise, she informed me that she'd enrolled Scribble and me at Wal-Bark, a dog training school sandwiched between a real estate office and a shoe repair shop, across the street from the discount store with the very similar name.

In the blink of a cold, parental eye, my research into paranormal communications was being shanghaied by eight weeks of studying "down," "sit," "stay," "heel," and "come."

To my further astonishment, the proprietor and trainer of Wal-Bark turned out to be none other than the ubiquitous ghost of Sam Walton, who by now, of course, I knew by sight, although this time he chose to introduce himself as Frank.

"How's it going?" I said, as Scribble growled the way he usually does at ghosts.

"Hey, Lawson," Frank replied. "What's happening?"

Jip's words exactly! I thought, momentarily taken aback by the coincidence.

If it *was* a coincidence!

Hmmm, I thought. *This is getting interesting.*

But it wasn't interesting to Scribble, for whom no spectral manifestation, no matter what it might have to say, could compete with a roomful of leaping, yapping puppies. Pulling like a seasoned sled dog in the frozen Yukon, his chest muscles straining, Scribble dragged me inside.

The Wal-Bark dog training center consisted of a narrow room with a scuffed and dusty checkerboard tile floor. Owners were asked to sit on metal folding chairs while their dogs ran around in circles beside them, tethered by six-foot leashes to snap hooks mounted on the wall.

Half a dozen puppies had showed up for opening

night: a sheltie; a bloodhound; a chocolate Lab; a beagle; a shaggy, mixed-breed miniature; and Scribble.

"An obedient dog can live for twenty years," Frank announced. "A dog that thinks for itself isn't likely to die of natural causes. What y'all are gonna learn in my class is how to replace y'all's mutt's outmoded instincts with mankind's superior knowledge."

Uh-oh, I thought. *Scribble's not going to like this.*

But I'd forgotten how long-winded "Frank"—or "Johnson," or "Sam," or whatever he wanted to call himself—could be. As he droned on with his presentation of the curriculum, Scribble got acquainted with the dog tied up next to him, a tan and white female beagle named Lady Osborne.

Never had I seen Scribble so excited. He spun around, rolled over, and jumped up and down like a toddler at his best friend's birthday party. Despite being restrained, Scribble nipped and tumbled with the playful beagle until their leashes became woven together.

At this point, I agreed with Lady Osborne's owner—an easygoing young man named Jeff—that the only thing to do was set the puppies free while we worked to untangle the snarl.

Immediately, Scribble and Lady Osborne started chasing each other up and down the room, skidding to a stop at each end, flipping around, and leaping over each other like circus acrobats.

The other dog owners, seeing how much fun these two

students were having, immediately followed suit, and the first night of dog training class concluded with "Frank's" introductory remarks being drowned out by yipping, yapping, yelping puppies.

"Any questions?" Frank asked at the end.

"I have one," I said, aware that this was the first time Scribble had been around his own species since the day Jip had plucked him from his litter. "Which do dogs like better, people or other dogs?"

"Well, now," Frank replied, "that's a dern good question. I reckon the answer depends on the dog's situation. Thousands of years ago, according to the experts, clever wolves befriended early human beans as a strategy for stayin' alive. But when it comes to what's in their hearts, a dog's prob'ly no diffrint from anybody else. He's prob'ly gonna be more at home with kin. In other words, blood is thicker than what's in the water dish."

Hmmm, I thought.

I didn't doubt what Frank was telling me, but to consider the power of family ties was disconcerting. It brought to mind one of Jip's relatives—her cousin, Chuck.

Have I mentioned Chuck?

At sixteen, Chuck not only could drive a car but owned one, a shiny black two-door coupe with a spoiler on back and a license plate that read 2KOOL4U, a clue to Chuck's primary interest—himself.

When he wasn't bragging about his accomplishments

—on the football field, in the stock market, at the high school dance—Chuck enjoyed making fun of other people, imitating their voices, their gestures, and their mannerisms, including mine.

Although the housebound Jip found her cousin highly amusing, I couldn't stand the guy. Many was the time I turned around and went back home because Chuck's car was parked in Jip's driveway.

"Chuck's a blowhard," I told her. "He has no redeeming qualities."

"Don't be harsh, Lawson," Jip admonished me. "He's just acting that way to conceal his vulnerability."

"Well," I observed, "it's working."

It wasn't so much that Chuck was a meathead, or that he was older, richer, better-looking, and more experienced than me. It was that as Jip's mother's brother's firstborn son, Chuck had a connection to Jip that I could never have: genes.

The only people I shared genes with were Cornelia and Buzz.

Scribble was reluctant to part from Lady Osborne. The two of them were acting like long-lost soul mates, birds of a feather, peas in a pod, kissing cousins.

Annoyed with it all, I wrestled Scribble to the door. Sam Walton—or, I should say, "Frank"—shook his head at us as we left.

"Don't y'all get discouraged, now," he advised. "Them terriers are mostly like that."

Haunted House

Having exhausted himself at school, Scribble slept through the night. Even when the morning light began leaking through the blinds, he stayed curled up on the pillow. Not until the strident voices of Cornelia and Buzz echoed through the air ducts did Scribble at last open his eyes.

"How could you be so clumsy?" Cornelia hollered.

"The person you should blame is the person who put it there," Buzz retorted. "I mean, come on—a fish bowl balanced on top of a grandfather clock? It was bound to happen."

"You knocked it off on purpose!" Cornelia shouted. "You've always hated my fish!"

"That's ridiculous!" Buzz replied. "I didn't even know it was there."

"So, you admit it!" Cornelia snapped. "You weren't paying attention!"

As their spat continued, I peeked into the room to see a blue *Beta splendens*—a Siamese fighting fish—on the floor, flopping and gasping in a puddle amid sharp-edged shards of glass. With neither of the combatants paying it the least attention, I swooped in, scooped it up, and dropped the desperate creature into a glass of water, a mission accomplished in the time it took Scribble to yawn, stretch, and amble to the front door.

"Okay," I told him. "We can go now."

Once outside, Scribble relieved himself in the grass, barked at the trash cans lined up on the curb, and sifted through mulch in the garden, picking out a piece that was big enough to chew. Thinking he'd enjoy a game of fetch, I pried the wood from his mouth and tossed it into the yard next door, where it landed a few feet from the For Sale sign.

Jip's house had been unoccupied for some time. The unusually long dry spell, extending from early fall all the way through winter, had left the lawn patchy, brittle, and khaki brown. The bushes, once luxuriant evergreens, had been reduced to prickly husks—mere memories of their former selves. And something about the house itself—a dullness to the paint, a gray, gritty film on the windows, a wobbly porch railing, a rusted downspout—warned prospective buyers to stay away.

It was as if Jip's house were in mourning.

But such cues don't apply to dogs, especially dogs like Scribble. Wherever there's something interesting to sniff, Scribble will gladly go.

This time, the little terrier's nose led him along an invisible trail around Jip's house, where he paused at a pair of rosebushes by the back patio. On one of them, a yellow rosebud, mummified by the elements, clung stubbornly to a lifeless branch. Trailing out from it, a few strands of what appeared to be an old spider web rippled in the breeze, like a tattered flag raised by Lilliputians.

Kneeling to examine the fluttering filament, I suddenly

had the disturbing feeling that I was being watched. The next moment, I could swear I heard someone call my name.

"Lawson," a voice seemed to whisper. "Look inside."

Startled, I stood up and looked around.

I could see no one.

Scribble growled and began digging at the bush, his nails slicing into the earth like tiny plows, flinging dirt to the right and left and up against his dappled belly.

Above his head waved the spider web material, shiny and phosphorescent, sort of like fairy floss, or cotton candy, and a whole lot like the strange substance we'd encountered by the pond.

Uh-oh, I thought.

"Keep away, Scribble," I warned him. "You remember what happened the last time."

But having completed only one hour of obedience school, Scribble was a long way from having the attributes of a graduate. Ignoring my command, he poked his snout into the rosebush and promptly disappeared.

"Holy smokes!" I cried out in alarm, lunging to where he'd just been.

What happened next is not entirely clear to me. Even now, I have difficulty making sense of the details. I definitely recall a loud hissing sound, like when you open a can of Pringles, but it lasted a lot longer than that, so I suppose it was more like a genie escaping from a bottle or magic lamp. Then, I'm ninety-nine point ninety-nine percent certain that I was dematerialized, although only briefly, after which I was teleported from Jip's backyard into an empty room—well, not completely empty: Scribble was there waiting for me.

We hadn't traveled far. Outside the sliding glass door, which, curiously, was open about six or eight inches, a crisp brown leaf from one of the rosebushes fluttered to the ground. Inside, dust bunnies drifted in shafts of sunlight.

Somehow, against all logic, Scribble and I had entered Jip's house.

Once again, the whisperer summoned me: "Hey, Lawson, in here."

It seemed to be coming from Jip's room.

Yikes! I thought. *Am I ready for this?*

Sharing my apprehension, Scribble held back, his white hair standing up on end.

A thousand thoughts raced through my mind, all of them having to do with Jip.

What if she was waiting for me in the next room?

I knew I should be overjoyed to see her, but what if after all this time away from her earthly body, she—how can I put this delicately?—*didn't look like herself?*

A feeling like real fear rushed to the surface.

What if these sightings, these messages, these sounds, that I had been so quick to attribute to Jip were nothing but my overactive imagination?

What if I was afflicted with wishful thinking?

Or more worrisome still, what if what was happening was some sort of evil trick and I was about to fall victim to dark forces, to a menacing, malicious, multiheaded beast from the beyond?

I didn't know what to do.

My experience couldn't help me, and my instincts could very well be out of date, like those of a dog descended from prehistoric wolves, trying to figure out what to do with a TV remote control.

A rattle at the front door put a stop to my dithering.

"Someone's coming!" I announced to Scribble. "We'd better hide!"

But in a house without a stick of furniture, hiding is something easier said than done. Dashing into the nearest closet, Scribble and I crouched down and gently closed the door.

"Shhh!" I told him. "Sit, stay."

To my surprise, Scribble did as instructed, quietly taking up the position of a sentry.

Although the closet no longer held anybody's belongings, the smell of shoes, boots, coats, hats, and gloves was still strong, a mix of must, dust, wool, perspiration, and perfume, suggesting that there's no such thing as a completely empty room.

Particles from former occupants expand to fill a space, an aromatic essence as distinctive as a signature, radiating from walls and baseboards and drifting like unseen phantoms in the air. I could sense Jip and her mother as if they were right there with me.

With his advanced sense of smell, I thought, *imagine what Scribble can detect!*

A voice came from the next room—not the whisper that I'd heard before, beckoning me to come inside, but a male voice, frustrated, angry, and loud.

"Where the devil can it be?" it questioned. "It's not like there's that many places to hide things!"

"*Grrr,*" Scribble sounded under his breath.

"Shhh!" I reminded him. "Be quiet."

From the next room, a door slammed and footsteps echoed down the hall, followed by another slamming door and distant, irate muttering.

Whoever was in Jip's house was going through the closets.

"Listen, Scribble," I whispered. "We've got to get out of here."

I pushed open the closet door a couple of inches and peeked into the room. The patio entrance was just a few feet away. For the moment, it seemed, the coast was clear, but a loud thud from the kitchen, followed by cursing, warned me that the opportunity for escape wouldn't last long.

Giving Scribble a tug, I dashed across the room and slid the glass door aside, making almost no noise at all. Unfortunately, the same was not true for Scribble. His collar tags—one the mandatory evidence of his rabies vaccination, the other offering his name, telephone number, and the tantalizing word *reward*—jingled like reindeer's bells on the roof.

"Hello?" the voice from the kitchen called. "Is somebody there?"

With a burst of speed that only the truly guilty can attain, Scribble and I sprinted around the corner and across the yard, escaping into my house before the intruder could catch a glimpse of us.

Such hard-won anonymity cuts both ways. Panting behind my front door, with Scribble running up and down the hall in hopes of continuing our entertaining footrace, it occurred to me that I never saw the intruder either.

Who was he? I wondered.

Or, should I be asking, *what was it?*

Tricks of the Mind

If dreams are a wish your heart makes, which organ is in charge of nightmares? Can your liver make you so scared that you can't get out of bed? Your spleen? Your pancreas? Perhaps it will turn out that nightmares are the primary function of the appendix.

Someone should conduct research on this.

I woke up in the wee hours of the morning, freezing cold yet too overcome with terror to shiver. A long, complicated nightmare about faceless killers in my house had me more scared than I've ever been before. Its plot details can't begin to convey the horror of that moment. Suffice it to say that never, ever have I felt so helpless. I thought about crying out to Buzz and Cornelia, but so great was my fear that even if I'd believed that one of them might respond, which I did not, my lips were too tense to move.

Scribble must have sensed my paralysis. Asleep at my feet, he stirred himself just enough to tunnel up through the covers and snuggle beside me, laying his head on my immobile hand to comfort me, not with words but with his body heat and chin whiskers.

Slowly, like ice retreating from the surface of a pond, my dread began to melt away, starting at the edges.

Good dog, I thought, not daring to speak. *Good dog.*

The hours between two a.m. and sunrise are prime thinking time. Understandably, all of my attention was on the trauma I'd just been through. The nightmare had unreeled like a movie, starting with foreboding encounters and ending with a frightening chase scene from which the only escape was to find a way to wake up.

At one point, when he's got me cornered in the basement, one of the killers demands, "Hand over the package, kid."

"What package?" I squeak in reply. "I don't know what you're talking about."

"Don't play dumb with me," he says. "I know you have it."

The voice, deep and threatening, is that of Jip's cousin Chuck.

It's while recalling this that I realize it's the same voice that called from the kitchen when Scribble and I were making a break for it in Jip's empty house.

How do I know that? I marveled.

How was I able to identify the intruder later, when I couldn't do it at the time?

The brain must have a mind of its own.

It must work something like this: When we're asleep, our subconscious mind is wide awake, processing all the billions of bits of information gathered by our senses from throughout the day, searching its dark, gooey, convoluted database for trends, patterns, sequences, similarities, and matches. Once in a while, when it does manage to put two and two together, the subconscious leaves a memo for the conscious mind headed, WHILE YOU WERE OUT.

In this case, the mental note read, *Chuck is looking for something that belonged to Jip.*

It was the only logical explanation.

Scribble, his concern for me mounting, began licking my hand.

"Thanks, pal," I whispered, scratching his hard, maraca-size noggin. "You're the greatest."

To direct me, Jip had probably deployed a whole platoon of fellow phantasms, recruiting sympathetic ghosts wherever she could find them, enlisting the aid of the unknown and the famous alike. Her only requirement must have been that they be capable of materializing to deliver me a message.

"Lawson, in here," Jip had said, for now my subconscious mind advised me that hers was the voice that whispered from the house. "There's something in here that was overlooked—something that you need to see."

The implication was clear: whatever had been left behind when Jip's mother moved away, I had to find it before Chuck did.

The race was on.

Songs and Laughter

My father was singing.

"Oh, what a beautiful morning . . . oh, what a beautiful day . . ."

In a house where joy was a stranger, this was unusual behavior.

"What's with you?" I asked, splashing milk on my cereal and the tabletop, as well.

"Not a thing," he replied cheerfully. "Just going on a brief business trip."

"Hmmm," I said.

My father's job rarely required travel. Nor, thankfully, did it require singing. Buzz liked to say that the only way he could safely carry a tune was in a suitcase.

Unlike Jip.

Jip had a lovely voice. What it lacked in power it made up for in smoothness and clarity. Her favorite songs were dreamy love ballads that were popular years before either of us was born. Hearing Jip sing "Unforgettable," for example, was like listening to a mountain stream slipping over water-worn rocks through a flower-dotted meadow.

In my mind, I could hear her voice.

Why couldn't I see her face?

I shook off the gloom that was trying to get me down. *C'mon, Lawson,* I told myself. *You have work to do.*

There was the usual long list of household chores; Scribble's homework and night class; and, now, the situation that had developed next door.

Where could you possibly hide something in an empty house? And how do you go about finding it when you don't know what it is?

Scribble entered the kitchen with his doll in his mouth, signaling his desire to play a particularly aggressive form of fetch.

The doll, a pink, threadbare, soft-bodied Barbie, had been a gift from Jip. I called the skinny, grinning plaything "Dog-Bone Barbie."

Scribble liked for me to throw Dog-Bone Barbie across the room so he could bring it back for me to hold while he fought furiously to tear it from my hands. Understandably, by now Dog-Bone Barbie was a wretched sight. Only a few straggly wisps of blond hair remained, its head was turned backward, both of its plastic hands had been chewed off, and the stringy stuffing from one leg dangled through a gaping hole in its knee.

"Poor Barbie," I said. "You're not long for this world."

With the suddenness of a sneeze, the gloom returned.

Not long for this world?

That was Jip's line.

As the day progressed, things got no better. Jip's house

was locked up tight, and the wall-defying ghost goo, previously as abundant as fleas in summertime, apparently had dried up and blown away. The rosebushes were clean. So were the pine trees by the pond. By nightfall, having accomplished absolutely nothing, I was feeling pretty glum.

Walking along the sidewalk to training class, I let out a long, loud sigh.

Scribble shot me a quizzical look, as if to say, "What's the matter, Lawson?"

"Sorry, Scribble," I told him. "I'm guess I'm just a little dispirited."

But no sooner had I spoken than I laughed at my own choice of words.

Dispirited, I thought.

Dis-spirited. De-phantomed. Un-ghosted.

Ha!

Trotting along at my side, Scribble laughed too.

Some people may doubt that dogs are capable of such a feat, but there's ample evidence to support my observation. First of all, it's a well-known fact that laughter is contagious. One person giggles in study hall, and it's not long before the entire classroom is erupting in guffaws— everyone, that is, except the teacher.

It's also been documented that chimpanzees laugh, most often as a result of being tickled. Researchers report that laboratory rats sometimes appear to laugh too, although what they're laughing at is not fully understood. Their captors, perhaps?

All of this has led some scientists to conclude that laughter is a widespread trait among mammals, an instinctive form of social bonding. The reason this fact is not better accepted, however, is that different species tend to laugh in different ways. In Scribble's case, his laugh was a throaty expelling of air that to a less attuned ear could be mistaken for a cough.

I knew better, of course.

Dispirited, I thought. *Good one!*

"Huh, heh, huh, heh, heh," Scribble responded.

At Wal-Bark, Sam Walton, still calling himself "Frank," was outside the door, shaking hands with dog owners from the early class, just breaking up. Except for the ball cap, he looked like a preacher after a Sunday morning service.

"What's wrong with that little rat terrier?" he asked, as Scribble and I tried to slip inside.

"Sense of humor," I explained.

"I'm not sure that's desirable in a dog," "Frank" said.

Once class got under way, it was a lot like before. Sit and stay took a back seat to "Frank's" long-winded speeches. As "Frank" reminisced about hunting quail with a black and white bird dog named Ol' Roy, Scribble romped with his friend Lady Osborne, occasionally exchanging nips with a newcomer to the group, a miniature pinscher named Buster.

"Interesting markings on your dog's back," commented Buster's owner, a woman wearing lots of jewelry. "Reminds me of ancient Egyptian letters—you know, those little pictures inside the pharaoh's tomb."

"Hieroglyphs?" I replied.

"The pharaoh didn't hire anybody," she corrected me. "His workers were slaves."

"Hmmm," I said.

"I find Egyptian history fascinating," she continued. "Especially the pyramids, with their secret passageways and hidden rooms stocked with food and treasure. So interesting. But how can you use supplies sealed behind walls of stone?"

"Ghost goo!" I blurted out without thinking.

"Gesundheit," Buster's owner replied, offering me a tissue.

When "Frank" reached the part in his story where Ol' Roy flushes out his final covey, he dabbed at his eyes with a cotton handkerchief and class concluded for the night. Like every dog story that ends with the passing of its hero, this one was sad, but not sad enough to overwhelm the notion of passing through walls to find valuable hidden objects.

"Excuse me," I said to "Frank," shaking his dry, wrinkled hand. "I was wondering if you could tell me where I might be able to find some ghost goo."

"Ghost goo?" he replied. "Why, Wal-Mart, of course. It's in health and beauty supplies, right in front of the pharmacy, just past hair color, on the second shelf from the bottom, next to the Dippity Doo."

"Thank you," I said. "You've been very helpful."

It was dark outside, and already past suppertime, but I

was pretty sure my mother wouldn't mind if I turned up a few minutes late. All I had to do was zip into Wal-Mart, grab the ghost goo, and pay for it. What could be easier?

The only problem was Scribble. As I've mentioned before, except for seeing-eye dogs, man's best friend isn't welcome inside Wal-Mart—a curious rule, given the founder's obvious affection for his own dog, Ol' Roy.

I'd have to smuggle Scribble in.

"Listen up," I told him. "There'll be no jumping, no wiggling, no biting, no barking—no disturbances of any kind. Do I make myself clear?"

Accepting the terms, Scribble licked my face.

The Wal-Mart Supercenter is open twenty-four hours a day. No matter when you arrive, cars, trucks, vans, and shopping carts are scattered over the oil-stained pavement like candy wrappers on a grade school playground. For some reason, the entrance is protected by concrete pylons sunk deep into the ground, as if Wal-Mart weren't a discount store but the United States embassy in Senegal, Saudi Arabia, or Singapore.

I helped myself to a free cart and lifted Scribble in. Obediently, he scrunched down on the wire bottom as I rolled us through the automatic sliding doors. We got no further than the talking gumball machine when an elderly woman in a blue smock held up her hand and said, "Sorry, no dogs."

"It's okay," I explained. "We just need a couple of items. I won't let him out of the cart."

"Sorry," she said again, more firmly this time. "Rules are rules."

"But—" I started to say.

"I'll watch him for you," a voice behind me interjected. "If you won't be too long."

I turned around to face a very tall, plain-looking woman with a warm but crooked smile. She was wearing a double strand of pearls, a long fur stole, and carried a black patent leather purse that was as big as a duffel bag.

"Such a handsome dog too," she added, in a loud, hooting sort of voice. "What's his name?"

"Scribble," I told her. "But I don't like to leave him anywhere."

"Here, Scribble, come here, boy," the woman whooped, a startling sound that reminded me of the distress call of the common loon.

Scribble put his paws on the edge of the cart and wagged his tail.

"Would Scribble like a treat?" the woman asked.

From her handbag, she produced a green dog biscuit. Instantly, Scribble gobbled it down and sniffed for more.

"We'll be waiting right here," she told me, picking Scribble up and giving him a hug. "You're a good dog, aren't you, Scribble?"

Scribble wiggled in delight.

"Well, all right," I agreed. "I'll just be a minute."

Although the ghost goo turned out to be right where I'd been told it was, it took me a few minutes to find the right section and then even longer to identify the product among the scores of bottles, tubes, jars, and cans of styling sprays, creams, foams, pumps, pomades, and gels.

Who in the world needs so many choices?

Further complicating my search was the fact that there was only one package of ghost goo left, a surprisingly small screw-top tin no bigger around than a half-dollar, sealed in a pilfer-proof cardboard-and-plastic sleeve labeled, EQUATE BRAND SPECTRAL ESSENCE (COMPARE TO GHOST GOO). FOR EXTERNAL USE ONLY.

I whistled when I saw the price. For such a smidge of product, it seemed very expensive—$17.96 for a quarter-ounce ("prepacked weight").

And in Wal-Mart, at that!

With tax, this one purchase would gobble up all but a couple of coins from the twenty-dollar bill my father had given me for emergencies.

Oh, well, I thought. *I'm not expecting an emergency.*

Don't bother saying it: Such thinking is at the heart of any number of stupid ideas. It would have made more sense to think of the exorbitant price as a warning to reconsider what I was doing.

I'm also struck by the irony that even when they come from a loner, stupid ideas tend to travel in packs. This was proven less than thirty seconds after I gave my emergency money to Wal-Mart and stepped outside to discover that the woman watching Scribble was gone.

Right before my eyes, I'd let my dog get kidnapped!

Here We Go Again

Where does a story begin? When you lose your best friend? Which time, the first time or the second?

In many ways, the unexpected loss of Scribble was no different from the gradual, anticipated departure of Jip. Whether slow or fast, gone is gone.

Heart-gripping panic, uncontrollable rage, unbearable sorrow, sharp, intense pain—it all comes surging forth as one complex emotion, boiling up from the depths with the force and fury of a volcano.

Maybe I should have started my narrative here, when I was at my lowest point, so I could present the illusion of a life of progress, instead of jotting down a jumbled heap of recollections as they come to me. But my life hasn't been a straight line, with one event leading inevitably to another. Instead, like a spiraled web, my past keeps returning, not repeating itself—not exactly—but imitating itself, as if it were trying out alternate scenarios.

As if it were mocking me.

Alone under the mocking lights of the Wal-Mart parking lot, my dog and my hopes for happiness gone, I was no longer sure what I believed.

Had I really walked among ghosts? Passed through walls and fences? Heard voices call my name while unseen hands carefully spelled it out in ink-stained script?

Or had I then, like now, allowed myself to be duped, victimized by a dying child's imagination, swept up in the foolish fancies of Jip's wishful thinking?

Tricked by ghost-lovers and dognappers alike.

Compelled to do something—anything!—to get my dog back, I hurried home and set to work as if Scribble had run away, staying up late to compose a classified ad for the newspaper and to create a stack of Lost Dog fliers to tape to streetlights and mailboxes.

Morning found me searching fields, ravines, and backyards all over town, knowing that the effort wasn't likely to produce results but afraid not to try.

In the afternoon, I visited the animal shelter, where I was moved by the tragic sight of so many misplaced pets. Finally, although I was sure it would be a waste of time, I placed a telephone call to the police.

"Sorry, but we don't search for dogs," the voice on the phone explained. "We're up to our armpits in cases involving people."

"Okay," I said. "Then how about finding the woman who took my dog?"

"What did she look like?" he asked.

"Old, tall, gangly, weak chin, baggy eyes, thick lips, turkey neck, ratty hair, a voice like wind through a sewer pipe, and dressed like the owner of a thrift shop."

The policeman laughed.

"If I didn't know better, I'd say you're looking for Eleanor Roosevelt," he said.

"Who?" I asked.

"Never mind," he replied, chuckling. "We'll let you know if she turns up."

Although I wasn't unaccustomed to getting the

brushoff from adults, I still found the policeman's manner insulting. Clearly, he was one of those people who assume that whenever a concern is spoken by a child, it must be something trivial.

Jerk, I thought.

But while tacking a Lost Dog poster to the bulletin board in the public library, I was seized with an impulse to follow up on his wisecrack.

A computer inquiry using the name Eleanor Roosevelt yielded more than three hundred and fifty references.

Holy cow! I thought.

I chose a one-volume pictorial history of the United States, largely because its editors had thoughtfully confined their coverage of each major topic to a single page, most of which they devoted to a photograph or a map. The accompanying words were little more than captions.

Flipping to page two hundred and sixty-seven, I was flabbergasted by the black-and-white picture that met my eyes. Dressed in a long woolen coat and wearing a metal helmet on her head, a woman with hands like a man's, lips like a frog's, and dark, sunken eyes was talking to a soot faced group of workers in a coal mine.

This, the text explained, was the most admired woman of her age, wife of the only four-term president of the United States, champion of the downtrodden, friend to the friendless, tireless worker for world peace, an "ugly duckling" made beautiful through a lifetime devoted to selfless acts: Anna Eleanor Roosevelt, born 1884, died 1962.

Holy Toledo! I thought.

You could have knocked me over with a library card!

What was so astonishing was not that the woman in the picture was deceased, nor that she had been in that condition for the better part of two generations, for by now such otherworldly occurrences were becoming commonplace. No, what I found surprising wasn't that I'd seen a ghost, but that the ghost I'd seen was judged by history to be one of humanity's finest people.

I shook my head in wonder.

If she's such a nice lady, I thought, *why did she steal my dog?*

Loose Ends

The biggest difference between a story that's made up and one that actually happens to you is loose ends.

In fiction, it's all tidied up by the time you reach the end. In real life, few things ever get resolved. Even death fails to have the last word, especially if you believe that some part of us survives our earthly bodies.

Jip had died. Scribble was gone. My parents had quit quarreling—at least, so long as Buzz was out of town. Enigmatic messages, both written and spoken, were arriving from the Other Side, presumably from Jip.

Chuck was searching for something hidden inside Jip's mother's house. Spirits were materializing in substantial numbers, then vanishing without explanation, except for

Sam Walton, who kept popping up everywhere, using various pseudonyms, and Eleanor Roosevelt, whose historical reputation for good deeds was in serious peril, as far as I was concerned. And unless I found Scribble soon, his tuition, prepaid for eight sessions, would be forfeited. Wal-Bark's policy was firm: no refunds.

From where I stood, I saw nothing but loose ends, with no way to tie up any of them, unless the task could be accomplished with a tiny, overpriced tin of commercial ghost goo.

As it so often does, the situation seemed hopeless. Even a sudden rise in temperature, marking the long-awaited changeover from winter to spring, failed to cheer me.

The telephone was ringing when I walked in the door.

"We found your cat," a voice said. "Please come get him."

"I didn't lose a cat," I explained. "I lost a dog."

"Well," the voice replied, "do you *want* a cat?"

The moment I hung up, the phone rang again. A professional pet finding service was offering to search for Scribble for two hundred and seventy-five dollars a day, plus expenses.

"Thanks anyway," I said.

The telephone continued to sound. One caller wanted to express his sympathy, saying he used to have a dog that looked just like Scribble, except for his coloration, his breed, and his face. A woman said she was glad my dog was gone because she'd seen it pooping in her yard. A kid asked if I were offering a reward, and, if so, would it be paid in cash. A pet store manager offered to sell me a new dog at a twenty percent discount. One caller barked at me before disconnecting. Another quoted a passage from the Bible. Still another hung up as soon as I answered the phone. And so it went until bedtime, with the greedy, the isolated, and the seriously deranged taking turns dialing my number.

Clearly, it doesn't always pay to advertise.

It was shortly before five o'clock the next morning when the telephone woke me from a dream of falling through space.

"What?" I answered.

"Lawson?" a woman's voice inquired. "Is that you?"

"Who is this?" I asked.

"I'm so sorry for the worry I must have caused," she replied, her voice like an enormous woodwind instrument in the clumsy hands of a beginner, "but I waited as long as I could. What kept you?"

"Who *is* this?" I asked again, my irritation undisguised.

But, of course, I knew the caller's name.

"Mrs. Roosevelt," I continued, "what have you done with Scribble?"

"He's such an adorable little fellow," she replied. "And so feisty! Wherever did you find him?"

"Listen, lady," I snapped, "I don't give a flea's butt about your opinion of my dog. I just want him back—get it? And I want him back *now!*"

The response to my outburst was a prolonged silence.

76

"Please," I added.

"Meet me next door," she instructed, "in exactly one hour. And this time, don't be late."

Consistent with the condition of the caller, the line went dead.

After showering, dressing, and downing a bowl of cereal, I was disappointed to discover that I still had half an hour to go. Not enough time to clean my room. Too long to sit and watch the clock.

I picked up my latest purchase from Wal-Mart, intending to check the contents. To my consternation, however, I found it impossible to tear the thick, plastic outer packaging, and my scissors, designed for cutting paper, proved as ill suited to the task as my fingers.

Digging around in my desk drawer, amid old keys, nail clippings, rubber bands, miscellaneous plastic parts, broken wristwatches, and worthless pennies, I came across my long-lost Swiss army knife.

Aha! I thought. *This ought to do the trick.*

The Swiss army knife has got to be one of mankind's greatest inventions, ranking right up there with the triple-action toothbrush, the electronic garage door opener, and the self-inking return address stamp.

Only three and a half inches long, my Swiss army knife hid a complete toolbox in its bright red case, including tweezers, a pick, scissors, a file, a corkscrew, a saw, a pair of screwdrivers, an awl, a bottle opener, and knife blades of various lengths. The only problem with such a well-equipped, compact instrument is that you can never be sure exactly which tool you're pulling out, which was why, when I succeeded in making a hole in the hard plastic, I also managed to puncture my hand.

"Dang!" I said, plunging my palm into running water to stop the bleeding. "Dang and double dang!"

After that, I searched all over the house for the Band-Aids, finally locating them on a shelf in the laundry room, where no doubt the last emergency had occurred. By this time, the bleeding had stopped by itself.

I then returned to extracting the ghost goo from the package. This required using the saw tool to hack a circular hole the size of a door to a bluebird house. With two fingertips, I lifted the tiny tin out and carefully unscrewed the lid.

In its texture, the Equate brand spectral essence was familiar—gossamer and sticky, like the substance I'd encountered in neighborhood trees and rosebushes—but unlike the subtle scent of natural ghost goo, the aroma from this man-made concoction was highly pungent, reeking of concentrated, synthetic patchouli oil.

This better be the right stuff, I thought.

I rubbed a tiny dab onto the back of my hand. Immediately, my arm tingled all the way to my elbow, then disappeared.

Dang! I thought. *I should have insisted on a name brand.*

From the upstairs bedroom, my mother's alarm clock began to emit a steady, pulsing *beep-beep-beep,* which was followed by a loud curse and a splintering crash.

Now what? I thought.

As my teachers at school would be happy to confirm, here's a problem that I have with so many things:

Distractions.

With the best of intentions, I start out doing one thing, then something unexpected intervenes. Frequently, this is followed by yet another detour, and another, until soon I've forgotten what it was that I first set out to to do.

Until it all comes back to me like a burp.

In this case, after Cornelia had apparently calmed down and stepped into the shower, I remembered that I had to see a woman about a dog. How could I have forgotten about Scribble? Unfortunately, I was now three minutes late.

Panic gripped me. Three minutes. Did it matter?

Who knows what time means to a ghost?

Pulling on my jacket, I saw that my left arm had now disappeared all the way to the shoulder.

With the tin of artificial ghost goo in my jeans pocket, I raced next door to Jip's mother's house and slipped inside. The time, according to the clock on the built-in range, had advanced to 6:05.

There was no evidence of Mrs. Roosevelt and Scribble. Had I missed them?

Goodness knows, the woman didn't wait long at Wal-Mart. Was it possible they'd already been here and gone?

Three lousy minutes! Why, that's less time than it takes to sing "Unforgettable."

Inwardly, I kicked myself. Outwardly, such action

appeared to be the limit of my capabilities. Passing by the mirror in the bathroom off the kitchen, I saw that my entire upper body had disappeared. Only my lower legs and feet remained visible.

Obviously, I thought, *this isn't regular ghost goo.*

Suddenly, inches from where I was standing, the door from the garage began to open.

Yikes! I thought. *It's too late to hide.*

In a single motion, I smeared more ghost goo on my shoes and shins, kicked the tin behind the wastebasket, and hoped for the best. Half a second later, I found myself eyeball to eyeball with Chuck.

Interestingly, however, despite being close enough to hear me breathe, Chuck gave no indication that he could see me, although his nose wrinkled involuntarily at the strong, distinctive scent of patchouli. Apparently, the double application of Wal-Mart's brand of ghost goo had rendered me completely invisible.

Keeping a careful distance, I followed Chuck down the hallway to Jip's room, where he sat in the middle of the floor with his legs crossed, removed what looked like a diary from his shirt pocket, and clicked open a ballpoint pen.

"I'm here," he announced softly. "You may proceed."

At first, Chuck's words gave me a start—I thought he was talking to me—but when I tiptoed around to take up a position silently in a back corner, I saw that his eyes seemed to be closed.

Chuck remained in a Buddhalike posture for a long time, unspeaking and unmoving, with nothing to break the stillness but the occasional muffled rush of a passing car outside. Then, just as my right foot began to tingle with pain, he jerked upright, grunted loudly, and collapsed from within, like dirty laundry dropped on the floor. With pen pressed to paper, he started to scribble furiously, stringing together long, spaghettilike letters into a single, extended word.

Slipping noiselessly behind him, I leaned over his shoulder to read: "Heylawsonwhatshappening."

"Holy cow!" I exclaimed right out loud.

Despite my outburst, Chuck remained as stiff as a display in a dinosaur museum. But though *he* didn't notice that I was in the room, given what he'd written down, Jip obviously did.

She must be nearby, I concluded.

"Jip," I whispered. "If you can hear me, tell me, how are you doing?"

Chuck's fingers gripped the pen so tightly that his knuckles went white, as if he were fighting to keep the writing instrument from leaping off the page.

"Not bad, Lawson," he scrawled on Jip's behalf. "All things considered."

All right! I thought excitedly. *Now we're getting somewhere!*

"Jip," I said, continuing the interview. "Can I see you sometime?"

For several minutes, there was no sign of a reply. It was as if Radio Chuck had simply gone off the air. Then without warning, his perfect teeth began to chatter, goosebumps appeared on his muscular arms, and, rocking back and forth on the floor, the cousin-turned-medium started to shiver and moan.

"Watch the movie," he spelled out in wobbly, otherworldly letters that overlapped one another and crowded the edges of the page.

Interesting, I thought.

But Chuck had another surprise up his sleeve, so to speak. Returning his notebook to his pocket, he let out a sneeze as loud as a train whistle, an alarming and explosive report that sent his head recoiling backward as a ghost the size of a full-grown guinea pig flew from his nose.

"Aiii!" I screamed.

Glowing like a campfire and shaped like a cloud, the compact phantom struck the floor and shot up to the ceiling, where it hovered briefly overhead before dissolving into the atmosphere around it.

"Great mother of Zeus!" I cried.

Meanwhile, unperturbed by his involuntary service as a mobile apparition launcher, Chuck stood up, walked to the garage, climbed into his sports car, and drove away. As his car turned the corner, the effect of the tinned ghost goo faded and my visibility returned.

Watch the movie, I repeated to myself.

No doubt, I concluded, Jip was referring to *Topper Returns,* the black-and-white near-classic about the murder-mystery-solving ghost. Doubtless, something in it explained how I might be able to see the face of my departed friend.

I made a mental note to investigate it at my earliest opportunity. In the meantime, in spite of the unexpected breakthrough, I had to deal with more pressing matters:

What had become of Mrs. Roosevelt and Scribble?

Sometimes, you can wonder about things for the longest time and the answer never comes—and not just big, cosmic issues, either, such as whether there's life on other planets, why you were born, or or the reason why girls act the way they do, but routine stuff too, like the ingredients in pimento cheese spread, and what actually happened to the fifteen dollars you forgot and left in your pants pocket yesterday.

But if nothing else, life is full of surprises. Not ten seconds after I pondered the whereabouts of my dog, Jip's mother's doorbell rang.

"Coming!" I called.

When I opened the door, there on the rotting welcome mat was Scribble, lying on his side and busily licking his private parts.

"Scribble!" I shouted. "Am I glad to see you!"

Yipping happily, he leapt into my arms and slobbered on my face. The fact that I let him do it tells you a great deal about how much I love my dog.

Changes

Love may not be blind, but it's nearsighted enough to need glasses.

Several days passed before I noticed how much Scribble had changed. For one thing, he was bigger than before. Though he was still trim and muscular, when I weighed him on the bathroom scale (a feat that requires weighing the two of us, then myself, and calculating the difference), he registered a surprising seventeen pounds. And while he had the same unique pattern of black markings on his back, his formerly smooth hair had grown thicker, longer, and rougher, into a coarse, scruffy, uneven type of fur known as a "broken" coat.

At first, I thought Mrs. Roosevelt might have switched dogs on me, but discarded that notion because, face it, I'd know Scribble anywhere. So, naturally, it then crossed my mind that the woman might have messed around with time, since in the forty-eight hours that he was gone, Scribble appeared to have aged by several months.

And that wasn't the strangest thing.

The first time it happened, we were walking in the woods. It was an unusually warm afternoon, with hawks overhead and turtles riding the current in the creek. Scribble, experiencing his very first spring, was sniffing everything in sight—tiny flowers blooming close to the ground, thick tufts of wild onions sprouting by the path, fallen logs rich with the rot of summers past.

All of a sudden, a butterfly, pale blue and no

bigger than a fingernail, somersaulted through Scribble's field of vision, and Scribble was off, leaping and snapping in the air, and jerking the leash out of my hand.

"Hey!" I burst out. "Get back here!"

Scribble, of course, ignored my shout, so I switched to something a little friendlier.

"Here, boy," I called, adding a short, sharp whistle. "Come here, now."

It must have been the whistle that did it, because it was when I inserted two fingers in my mouth and blew a perfect piccolo high G that Scribble suddenly stood up on his hind legs, held his paws out in front of him, and proceeded to twirl around and around like a stage-struck ballerina.

"Good grief, Scribble!" I gasped. "Have you no shame?"

But Scribble's dancing, while admittedly a startling sight, was not the mystery that it might have been. I'd been tipped off about this very phenomenon by Jip.

"It's called mesmerism," she'd explained, during one of those long, conversation-rich afternoons in her room. "We'd call it hypnotism today."

"Mind control," I clarified.

"Yes," she said, "but only to a very slight degree. During the heyday of the spiritualist movement, around the turn of the twentieth century, it was a common practice among professional mediums to mesmerize a volunteer for the amusement of the audience. Among the most popular stunts was to persuade an unwitting subject, on hearing a prearranged signal, to perform some embarrassing act: cry like a baby, bark like a dog, cluck like a chicken."

"And people actually did this?" I said.

"By the hundreds, apparently," Jip confirmed. "It was all the rage."

"But what does public humiliation have to do with communicating with ghosts?" I asked.

"It was a convincing way for a medium to demonstrate his powers," Jip explained. "Sort of a warm-up act, if you will, before the more controversial main event."

As Jip's well-researched words came back to me, it wasn't Scribble's circus dog antics that I found so surprising. No, the source of my astonishment was the underhanded behavior of certain beings from the Other Side. For some reason, after she succeeded in snatching him away from me, Mrs. Roosevelt had hypnotized my dog.

"C'mon, Scribble," I called. "Let's you and me go hunt rabbits."

"Yip," Scribble replied, standing with one hind foot in front of the other, his left forepaw raised over his head and his right one extended, a perfect execution of ballet's classic fourth position.

This is embarrassing, I thought. *How do I rehabilitate him?*

"To bring a subject out of a trance," Jip had explained to me, "typically, a medium would simply clap his hands. Not only did this serve to wake the dozing victim;

it had the added benefit of stimulating the audience to applaud, an important consideration, since so much of what we perceive as success is simply showmanship."

"You're a true fountain of knowledge, Jip," I said.

Jip sat up in her bed and beamed, flashing me a warm, affectionate smile, her eyes crinkling, her freckled nose flaring, her slender fingers tucking a wayward strand of hair behind one shell-shaped ear, and although I could see these close-up, intimate actions in my mind's eye as clearly as if they were happening in the here and now, it disturbed me that my memory couldn't reassemble the fragments into a fully recollected face.

Dang! I thought. *My best friend, and I can't remember what she looked like.*

Not surprisingly, since the information had come from the authoritative Jip, Scribble responded to the traditional mesmerist's antidote. As soon as he heard the clap of my hands he resumed his life as a dog, following me from room to room, curling up beside me when I sat down, napping nearby when I worked, and waiting at the front door for me to come home from school.

If anything, he dogged my steps more than before, no longer the fully independent creature he once had been. It was as if he was fearful of becoming separated again.

I couldn't even get him to go to dog school. Except for an occasional urgent dash to the tree in the front yard, no amount of tugging, commanding, begging, or bribing could persuade Scribble to leave the house.

Because of Mrs. Roosevelt's meddling, the brave,

adventurous Scribble had become a timid homebody and part-time dancer. And while there's no denying that danger is always lurking outside, to my way of thinking, the perils that now lay inside my house were equally daunting.

With the return of Buzz from his business trip, the war between my parents had resumed in earnest. Initially it was carried out in frosty silence, but soon something Buzz said or did tripped Cornelia's trigger, and the ensuing battle raged for the rest of the day. During lulls in the fighting, each of the combatants tried to enlist my support.

"Have you ever seen such a person?" Buzz asked.

"When you choose a companion, I hope you'll choose more carefully than I did," Cornelia advised.

Under these conditions, I wanted nothing to do with either of them. Whereas some children in homes like mine wonder if perhaps they were adopted, I was *hoping to be* adopted.

I considered using the store-bought ghost goo to hide out next door, but I realized that I'd left it inside the locked house, behind the wastebasket in the bathroom.

Rats! I thought.

As if that weren't enough, it began to rain—not one of those gentle spring rains that clear the air and coax forth flowers, but a cold, biting rain, the kind that on a moment's notice can turn into snow. It was as if winter had been called back onstage for an encore.

With bad weather outside and heavy weather inside, I retreated to my room, where, following Jip's recent written instruction, I began a second viewing of *Topper Returns*. Although nothing in it had changed since the first time I watched it, I did notice that its dapper, mustachioed star was named Roland Young, and that within the movie's shallow mystery and slapstick comedy was an instructional film about the three different forms of spirits.

Most commonly, it suggested, ghosts are invisible, occupying a wavelength outside the realm of earthly vision. This, it would seem, is their natural state.

Sometimes, however, under certain circumstances, departed souls become transparent, revealing themselves as see-through specters, free from gravity and other earthly constraints, capable of floating over their old haunts like smoke. These are the spirits that are the source of legend—the ghosts that go "boo!"

Finally, there are the fully manifested beings, spirits that look and act like you and me, except, of course, that they're no longer "alive," in the traditional sense of the word.

These are individuals on a mission—ghosts who must carry out some assignment before they can move on. The dead woman in the movie took this form with the reluctant man next door. Sam Walton and Eleanor Roosevelt had done the same for me. Doubtless, there were others hanging around that I hadn't yet identified.

Muffled by the whine of the air purifier, angry shouts drifted down from upstairs as the rain beat hard against my window. Climbing into bed with me, Scribble tunneled underneath the covers and snuggled against my leg. I reached down and gently rubbed his ribs.

"I know just how you feel," I told him.

Although a conversational cliché, the statement was true. The communication between my dog and me was complete. Whereas the divide between ourselves and other people, between men and women, husbands and wives, parents and children, and the living and the dead can be impossible to bridge, since his release from the traumatizing grasp of Mrs. Roosevelt, Scribble and I had become a fully realized pack of two. Despite our different species, we'd found a solution to our common plight: To keep chaos at bay, we had only to cling to each other.

Such closeness is not without its drawbacks, however. Habits, attitudes, and character traits are easily exchanged. Being a dog, Scribble was a master of procrastination. While lightning fast physically, philosophically speaking, to him, nothing was particularly urgent. As far as Scribble was concerned, it all could wait.

This explains why, even though I knew that eventually I'd have to deal with Chuck in order to communicate with Jip, and that I probably should be out looking for Sam Walton and Eleanor Roosevelt as well, I lay in bed with my head on a pillow, my eyes to the ceiling, and my right hand on the rib cage of a dog.

Succumbing to Scribble's seductive malaise, my ghost-hunting progress stalled. I became like the painter who does a dab a day.

What's the rush? I thought, my brain floating in a fog.

Jip's gone. What's time got to do with it now?

Shut away with an agoraphobic dog, I consumed a Jip-inspired diet of ancient poetry and old folks' music, nibbled aged imported cheese on butter-flavored crackers, and sipped glass after glass of blended berry punch. For days, my mind withdrew into its own happiness, creating, as the poet Marvell wrote, "far other worlds, and other seas; /Annihilating all that's made/ To a green thought in a green shade."

As the incomparable Nat "King" Cole crooned Jip's favorite tune, "Unforgettable," I luxuriated in the softness of my organic cotton blanket and took comfort in the warm proximity of my dog. Eventually, nothing else mattered. There was only Scribble, my memories, and me.

But nature abhors a vagrant, and as far as fate is concerned, an object at rest is a sitting duck.

It happened at midnight, the high noon of the Other Side. Starting as a faraway rumble, it was a distant, easily ignored event, not so much a sound as a sensation, weak and inconsequential, a faint vibration in my bones. Scribble, of course, was the first of us to respond, sitting up and growling, then barking angrily, in that severe, no-nonsense, beagle-esque voice of his, as if he'd detected a herd of brawny bison thundering our way.

All the while, sweet and low, the music continued to play:

> *Unforgettable, that's what you are.*
> *Unforgettable, though near or far.*

It was the air horn that gave everything away, the

raucous, ear-splitting release of turbocharged atmosphere blasting through a metal tube as big around as a bathtub drain.

It was the ghost bus, a vapor-powered city bus packed with passengers from beyond the pale, newcomers to their situation, vacant-faced, disoriented, confused, staring out the windows while clinging grimly to overhead straps, the twelve o'clock transit bursting through my bedroom walls and headed who knows where.

"My heavenly stars!" I shouted.

Incredibly, I recognized the bus driver, a handsome, dark-complexioned, lively-looking man with slicked down, wavy hair. Dressed in a tailored suit, with a thin black tie and a perfectly squared white handkerchief, he smiled broadly at me as the bus roared past.

It was Nat "King" Cole, the legendary singer, dead since 1965, Jip's personal favorite, and the one-time owner of the very voice I'd been listening to.

"It's in the basement," Nat "King" Cole called out above the din. "In a brown metal box."

As quickly as it came, the ghost bus was gone, in one wall and out the other. I could hear the sad moans of its riders as it rattled away in the distance.

"*Grrr,*" Scribble growled.

As if to say, "Good riddance."

A Face in the Crowd

These were hard times.

Cornelia and Buzz were bickering nonstop. School had become a series of minor setbacks. Scribble spent so much time sleeping, I worried he'd develop bedsores. And while the new information provided by Nat "King" Cole was surprisingly specific, so long as Jip's house remained locked, the late crooner's unexpected intervention only added to my sense of powerlessness.

At least the weather had improved. One Saturday morning, when Scribble's bladder rousted us out of bed, the temperature was already in the seventies, and according to the newspaper was expected to rise into the eighties by late afternoon. Once I was outside, the sight of tulips in the garden, dandelions on the lawn, and goldfinches twittering in the curbside tree worked to cure my long-festering gloom.

"How about it, Scribble?" I asked. "After breakfast, would you like to take a real walk?"

The little terrier lay at my feet and looked up at me with apologetic eyes.

"It's okay," I told him. "Neither one of us has been himself lately."

After considerable prodding on my part, midmorning at last found us on our way. Scribble's pace was a little off, perhaps from whatever had been bothering him, perhaps because he was unaccustomed to the heat, but to his credit he doggedly persevered, ambling, not trotting, down the sidewalk, poking his long, pointed face into fresh mounds of mulch, nibbling at every available bug.

Eventually our journey took us to the public soccer

fields, a sprawling expanse of close-cut grass and gravel parking lots that we could hear from two blocks away.

"Way to go, Britney!" a woman yelled.

"To the goal, Rachel," screamed another.

"Kick it, Ellie, kick it hard!" a man shouted.

Most athletic contests are spectator sports, but soccer, as the girls my age play it, is truly a spectacle. Like modern circus performers in a sunlit amphitheater, they were in constant motion, dazzling in their uniforms of lime green with lemon yellow stripes, crimson with magenta diamonds, purple with white squares, Day-Glo orange with hot pink stars.

On the sidelines, the fans, though few in number, were loudly appreciative of every effort, whether successful or not. Most of those who were watching sat in canvas chairs, but a few stood, including a familiar-looking man with an even more familiar-looking dog, a tan and white beagle whom I recognized as Scribble's dog school chum, Lady Osborne. An insistent lurch at the end of the leash told me that Scribble had recognized her too.

"Okay, boy," I told him. "Maybe it's just what you need."

While Scribble played hard with Lady Osborne, I watched the action on the field, but since I didn't know the teams, it wasn't long before my thoughts returned to Jip.

"What would you do if suddenly you won a million dollars?" she once asked me. "Would you move away?"

"I doubt it," I replied. "There's nothing wrong with

this neighborhood. The people are nice and you can easily walk to Wal-Mart. I'd probably just put the money in the bank."

"Don't be silly," Jip admonished. "Nobody keeps a million dollars in the bank."

"Well, maybe I would buy something," I admitted. "But I'm not sure what it'd be."

As we talked, Scribble chewed on a fuzzy slipper that he'd found on Jip's floor.

"Would you get another dog?" she inquired. "Someone for Scribble to play with?"

"Certainly not," I answered. "Scribble has me. I wouldn't want to subdivide his love."

"Oh, Lawson," Jip sighed, turning over in her bed, "you have so much to learn. Love isn't something that's divisible. Love can only be multiplied."

With their teeth locked in playful aggression on each other's necks, Scribble and Lady Osborne tumbled over and over in the grass.

That Jip. She knew something about everything.

A Different Point of View

"This toaster doesn't work right," Cornelia was saying.

"You just have to turn the dial," Buzz explained. "You adjust it to your bread."

"I shouldn't have to adjust it," Cornelia complained. "It should adjust itself."

"A lot of people like that feature," Buzz said.

"Well, I don't," Cornelia snapped. "I hate this stupid toaster!"

With her open hand, she slapped the appliance against the tile backsplash, kicked over a chair, and stormed out of the kitchen.

Although never quite so violently, Cornelia had expressed such sentiments before, and not just about the toaster. She also hated the can opener, the sofa fabric, the slope of the backyard, her car, the neighbors, our town, and, increasingly, it seemed, my father.

"I'm going to borrow Scribble for a while," Buzz said. "I'm sure he'd enjoy a nice long walk."

Later, when they returned, Scribble ran straight to his water bowl, then collapsed on the carpet. Buzz went upstairs and began packing two suitcases, one for him, and the other, it turned out, for me.

"This can't go on," Buzz decreed.

With Scribble sound asleep in the back seat, we drove through the night to my aunt's house.

My father's sister lives with her husband in the country, as far from city life as they could get, not on a farm but on twenty acres of rocky land that includes a house, a workshed, woods, a meadow, and a pond. They have no children but have filled that void with four dogs, five cats, and seven chickens, counting the rooster. When Scribble and I awoke the next morning in an upstairs bedroom, we felt as if a great burden had been removed.

For me, that burden was otherworldly spirits. My aunt and uncle's property, it seemed, was a ghost-free zone, with not a Sam Walton, Eleanor Roosevelt, Nat "King" Cole, or other dead celebrity in sight.

For Scribble, it was the leash. In the quiet, practically uninhabited countryside, he had no need for one. Few cars traveled up the gravel road, and my aunt's big dogs were happy to show a visiting terrier the ropes.

Scribble's initiation into the pack consisted of a perfunctory growl and sniff from Nate, a golden retriever mix, and a couple of laps around the yard with two aging border collies, Jules and Jim, after which he was handed over to a shaggy mongrel named Mutt, an affable, somewhat slow-witted dog whose mission in life was to search the woods for foul-smelling substances to roll in and eat.

It was Mutt who encouraged Scribble to bury his food dish in the meadow, and Mutt who taught him how to find four-leaf clovers.

The two of them would trot across the yard between the house and the shed, sniffing and circling like dogs do when they're looking for a place to poop, when suddenly Mutt would stop and point down, as if his nose were a divining rod, and there, underneath his broad, dripping nostrils, would be a lucky clover, its four round leaves as lush and symmetrical as could be.

Soon, Scribble was performing this feat on his own. In hardly any time at all, I filled the pages of a Webster's dictionary with dried, pressed, fragile good luck charms.

Needless to say, Scribble was having the time of his life. At last, he could just kick back and be a dog. The only problem was the chickens.

"He's welcome to stay here," my aunt said, "but I won't have him upsetting my birds."

Now, telling a Jack Russell terrier not to chase a chicken—one of Nature's least successful experiments—is like telling a kid not to eat chocolate chip cookies. What else could these stupid creatures be for?

In any event, my aunt said she had a sure-fire cure.

"It worked with Mutt," she explained. "And if it'll work on that one, it'll work on any dog."

What she did was tether Scribble to a stake outside the coop. From this vantage point he could see the chickens, smell the chickens, and experience the full range of empty-headed chicken behavior as one by one they taunted him, clucking and fluffing their feathers and strutting around as if they owned the place. Scribble strained against the rope, but to no avail, for the chickens, having been through this before, stayed just out of reach.

"No chickens," my aunt told Scribble firmly.

Taunting, cackling, the chickens shimmied in the dirt and flapped their nearly useless wings in Scribble's face.

"Those chickens," my father muttered, "remind me of Cornelia."

Scribble pulled harder.

"No chickens," my aunt said again. "No chickens."

Scribble looked at me, his big brown eyes wide with disbelief.

"Sorry, Scribble," I said. "Rules are rules."

Insistently, Scribble tugged again and again, and each time, my aunt repeated her command. Eventually, he gave one last halfhearted tug and sat down, his tongue draped over his teeth.

My aunt untied the rope.

"C'mon," I said to Scribble. "Let's go for a walk."

We headed off together down a gravel road. Beside the ditch, amid the tall weeds and poison ivy, blackberry bushes signaled future rewards with gently curved sprays of white flowers. Butterflies floated up like bubbles. By the time we'd rounded the bend, poultry was the last thing on our minds.

On a neighboring pasture, part of which had recently been cleared of trees, and separated from us by only a sagging, rusting barbed-wire fence, horses were exploring the rocky soil for tufts of grass.

One of them, a sorrel mare, put her head over the fence. Scribble froze in his tracks, dumbfounded. Had there ever been a dog so big? Instinctively, he stretched upward, and the two animals touched noses, Scribble wagging his stump of a tail and the mare switching her brushy broom from side to side.

When you forgo any use of words, it's easier to be friends.

I closed my eyes and breathed in the aroma of horses, their sweat, their breath, their rich manure, blended with the sap-wet sawdust from nearby newly felled trees, a sharp, fresh, natural odor that like the flip of an electric switch brought back a scene from my early childhood.

I'm at a pony ride at a county fair. An aging sway-backed palomino is trudging in circles, its broad back much too wide for my short legs. Fearful of falling, my fingers dig into the pony's thick, coarse mane. On the other side of a makeshift metal barricade, my mother and my father stand side by side, beaming. My mother calls my name. Her face is radiant. Her eyes sparkle with delight. She's holding my father's hand. Then she faces him and gives him a kiss.

Scent must be a doorway to memory.

Oh, Jip, I thought. *If only I could see you again.*

Country Music

In the city, time is controlled by schedules and clocks, but in the country, on an extended vacation from school, something more primitive runs the show, something involving songbirds and breezes and the predawn light.

Scribble and I were out of bed by five a.m. In the kitchen, wearing matching plaid nightshirts, my aunt and uncle were scrambling eggs, making toast, frying bacon, and in hushed whispers, so as not to disturb their house-guests, discussing plans for the day. Soon my father ambled in, sleepy-eyed and tousle-haired, pouring himself a steaming mugful of coffee and then disappearing for a while.

Back upstairs, while Scribble was outside with the big

dogs enjoying a breakfast of last night's leftovers, I began to make my bed, when, to my horror, I spied a tick crawling across the sheets. Immediately I called my aunt.

"What should I do?" I asked her.

"Oh, that's nothing," she replied, capturing the tiny black bug in a tissue and flushing it down the toilet. "The woods are full of them. It probably crawled off your dog."

Hmmm, I thought.

For a brief, disloyal moment, I questioned the wisdom of having such a close relationship with an animal, but when Scribble greeted me at the door with wiggles, leaps, and licks, I decided that a thorough brushing would settle our hygienic differences.

After breakfast, we piled into my uncle's car and drove to the farmers' market in town. Once a week, people from miles around bring stuff they've grown, baked, or canned, plus whatever portable livestock they've got extras of, and get together in a parking lot to trade. I was especially interested in the fancy pigeons—they looked as if they'd come from the jungle—but Scribble took a liking to the rabbits. He also ate a lot of unidentified substances that he found on the ground. On the way back home, while my aunt was cradling a plastic-wrapped coffeecake in her arms and my father was admiring the set of walnut bowls he'd bought, Scribble threw up in the back seat.

"Don't worry about it," my aunt said, patting my uncle on his knee. "Mutt does that all the time."

How different from my mother, I thought.

Later, the skies opened up and it began to rain—a real country gullywasher, with lightning crashing in the woods and thunder echoing across the fields. After a few hours of being housebound, I was getting restless.

"Here," my aunt said. "This will give you something to do."

From the back of a jumbled closet, she retrieved a cigar box. Inside were four half-used tubes of oil paint and two small brushes.

"But I'm not an artist," I protested. "Besides, I don't know what to paint."

"Just paint what you like," she replied, handing me a panel of canvas-covered cardboard. "If it's something you care about, perhaps others will too."

While my uncle played music on the stereo and Scribble dozed on the green leather sofa, I thought about the challenge at hand.

What I really wanted, more than anything, was to create a portrait of Jip, something that depicted her galaxy of tiny freckles and her mysterious Mona Lisa smile; however, not only was such a feat beyond my artistic ability, but I was still unable to mentally assemble the details of her face—not to mention, the paints I had were cadmium red, cadmium yellow, ultramarine blue, and titanium white.

What can you accomplish with a palette of preschooler's colors?

Scribble rolled over on his back, his feet sticking straight up in the air.

"Mutt sleeps like that sometimes," my uncle observed. "It's the strangest thing."

"That'll make a nice picture," I said.

For the next several hours, I worked on capturing the likeness of my dog at rest. First I sketched his outline with a pencil, wearing out the eraser to get his legs just right. Then I began mixing colors.

Theoretically, you can make any color you want out of red, yellow, and blue, but in actual practice this doesn't work. Cadmium yellow must have some orange in it, or ultramarine blue some purple, because when you mix the two together the only green you get is olive drab.

When the sofa I was trying to paint took on the lumpy, formless shape of a trash bag, I changed it to a hillside, an improvisation that necessitated turning the floor lamp into a tree, which, alone and bare like a telephone pole, seemed out of place, so I added a few more, dotting their tops with sage, tarragon, and mud-ocher leaves. My aunt's Oriental hall rug became a path lined with yellow flowers and purple vines. Slightly to the left and down from the center of the painting was the white face and pink, liver-spotted stomach of Scribble, his legs as stiff and upright as an inverted piano bench.

"Well, now that's interesting," my aunt said, looking over my shoulder. "A possum playing dead in the woods. Nice work, Lawson. You could sell that at the farmers' market."

Hmmm, I thought.

I stepped back to give my painting another look. That was when I realized that for the past hour and a half, the music that my uncle had been playing was Nat "King" Cole.

"Do you have 'Unforgettable'?" I asked.

"It's a ten-CD set of everything that Nat 'King' Cole ever recorded—more than two hundred songs arranged in chronological order," my uncle answered proudly. "We should be getting to 'Unforgettable' in a couple of hours."

"Be sure to call me when it comes on," I replied. "If I'm still up."

"Sure thing," my uncle said, turning his attention to Mutt, giving the animal's curly-haired back a vigorous rub. "Y'all are such a good dog, Mutt. Not real smart, but a good dog. Y'all never make excuses."

For some reason, that was when I realized that my uncle wears his baseball cap inside the house.

The Mystery of the Rotten Luck

My idyll in the country continued through blackberry season, when the dark, tart berries, bursting with juice, tumbled from their branches at a touch.

Scribble by now was fully grown, a muscular, solid little dog, fleet of foot and quick of mind, more confident and headstrong than ever.

My father had taken up cigars, smoking while meditating in a beechwood glider beneath a mimosa tree, the thin blue haze rising up through pink, ballerina-shaped blossoms.

My aunt taught me how to make jam. My uncle let me use his chain saw. Through my wanderings, I'd also come to know the routines of certain wildlife: a trio of owls, swarms of ruby-throated hummingbirds, dim-witted turtles drifting like discarded cartons in the pond, skinks sunning on a low rock wall.

The natural world suits me, I thought, *much better than the supernatural one.*

Night after night, with Scribble at my side, I slept without waking until morning. But finally the day came when we had to go back home. I felt it before I knew it. It was that sensation that you get on the night before a big test at school, that inwardly jumpy feeling bordering on dread.

I'd just come back from a walk with Nate, Jules, Jim, Mutt, and Scribble, and the way my father and my aunt stopped talking when we stepped out of the woods told me everything I needed to know.

"When are we leaving?" I asked.

"Tomorrow after breakfast," my father replied. "I'd like to get under way before it gets too hot."

"Okay," I said. "But Scribble's really starting to like it here."

"He's welcome to stay," my aunt said, kneeling to give him a hug. "There's always room for one more dog—especially such a cute one."

Shamelessly, Scribble licked her face.

The next day, just as the sun was topping the trees, we pulled onto the highway, first pausing for the light to change at the Wal-Mart Supercenter. Despite the early hour, the parking lot was filled with rusted vans and dusty pickups, some with hunting dogs in the back, their tongues hanging from their mouths.

Scribble pressed his nose against the window.

For the rest of the way, he slept, until we were about forty miles from home, when Scribble jumped up, barking in a low, anxious, throaty woof. The closer we got to home, the more agitated he became.

It has to be his ghost detector, I figured.

Concentrated in the city, the phantoms were radiating their spooky presence like escaped atomic energy. Invisible to the naked eye, but definitely trouble.

I wasn't sure I was ready for this.

My mother's car wasn't in the garage, which seemed to suit my father just fine. As we unloaded our gear and Scribble relieved himself in the front yard, a tapping sound from next door caught my attention. A real estate agent was installing a new sign in Jip's front yard: OPEN HOUSE SUNDAY.

That's tomorrow, I realized. *Maybe I'll finally get new neighbors.*

The shyer you are, the more important familiar faces become. If Jip had lived six blocks away, I'd never have spoken to her at all, but because she was right next door and I could see her every day from my window, eventually I had to make myself known.

I'll never forget my first glimpse of her. It was summer, shortly after she and her mother moved in. The two of them were outside in the bright sunshine, cleaning up an overgrown vegetable garden in their backyard. Dressed in white shorts and a cranberry top, Jip was bent over, wrestling a tall, prickly weedstalk from the soil. What I recall most vividly about that moment is that she had her back to me, so what I saw was mostly legs, long and skinny, topped by a spherical rear end. It was a picture much like the painted yard art that I've since seen out in the country. (Can this be why I have trouble remembering Jip's face? Surely not!)

In any event, that initial unexpected image made a profound impression on me. I felt my heart strangely warmed. A few days later, I crossed the driveway, rang the doorbell, and introduced myself.

"Hello," I said. "Welcome to the neighborhood."

"Oh, good grief," Jip replied. "It's the peeping Tom."

"Excuse me?" I said.

"Not likely," Jip countered. "You've been watching me."

"What makes you think that?" I asked.

"I don't think it—I know it," she retorted. "I've seen you standing at your window."

"You've seen me?" I repeated. "Inside my house?"

"That's right, buster," she said defiantly. "Lots of times."

"Then you're the one who's peeping," I declared.

From that awkward beginning, our relationship grew.

Since we were decreed by fate to live side by side, Jip's curiosity about me was no less intense than mine about her. But she held back her big secret for a long, long time, until one day it became impossible to withhold it any longer.

"What do you mean, 'sick'?" I said.

"I mean exactly what it means," she replied, not sounding in the least bit sorry for herself.

"How sick?" I asked.

"As sick as you can get," she answered.

"Oh," I said, still not fully understanding.

It was as if she'd told me she'd run away from the circus, or was raising chinchillas in her basement, or had a half brother who was a school librarian.

"Well, let's not let it affect our friendship," I said.

"Certainly not," she agreed.

What an idiot I am!

And what a mystery this life is. Especially the part concerning Jip. The unfairness, the obvious undeservedness, the cruel, capricious nature of one girl's being singled out through no fault of her own—that's what makes me so sad and so angry.

I won't bother asking why.

What would be the point?

I can't imagine any satisfactory answer.

. . .

Forgive me. I need a moment to collect my thoughts.

. . .

Look, what death feels like to the person who died obviously I don't know yet. But to the one who's been left behind, it feels like being hit by a runaway Chrysler on the sidewalk. It's not just that it hurts incredibly badly, but the pain goes on and on and on, without ceasing, and no matter how hard you try, you can't *not* think about it.

Perhaps I repeat myself.

There were times when I thought it would be better if I could just go to sleep one night and wake up the next day having forgotten not only Jip's face but everything—every shred of memory—about her.

But of course I couldn't do that. Jip was gone, yet at the same time she was always there, right in front of me. I had no place else to put her.

As I write this down, I'm crying. This doesn't happen very often, but when it does, I hug Scribble.

Scribble licks my eyes, my ears, my nose, my salty cheeks.

Still Life

The pattern, by now, had become a familiar one. Facts would be staring me in the face while I, preoccupied with other thoughts, would fail to see them for what they were, until, waking in the middle of the night, I would suddenly find everything to be clear. It was if a tape delay system had been installed in my brain.

In this case, I'd overlooked the obvious solution to the problem of Jip's locked house:

OPEN HOUSE SUNDAY.

"Holy smokes, Scribble," I said, sitting straight up in the darkness. "We don't even have to knock. We can just walk right in."

Scribble, clinging to sleep, scrunched himself against my stomach. The heat from his body was so soothing that I lay my head back on my pillow and prepared to shut my eyes.

That was when I noticed the man standing in my room.

There was a time when the appearance of a stranger under these circumstances would have sent terror surging through my heart, but in recent months, multiple encounters with various spirit forms had jaded me.

Neither was I certain that this particular apparition was a stranger. In the dim light from the window, he bore a certain resemblance to Roland Young, the long-forgotten star of the bargain DVD that I'd picked up at Wal-Mart.

"Are you Topper?" I asked.

"Sorry, no," the phantom said, stroking his mustache with his fingertips. He spoke with an accent, most certainly European, and probably French.

"Have you come to show me Christmas past and future?" I asked.

The phantom laughed. "No, no, no," he said, shaking his head. "It's about your painting."

On the other side of the room, propped up on top of

the dresser, my carefully crafted artwork of Scribble sleeping in the forest was a blank, shadowy, rectangular blur.

"I know it's not very good," I confessed. "It was my first try."

"It's not so bad," the ghost said reassuringly. "But here's a tip: Don't bother to mix your colors. Use them straight from the tube."

With that, he turned to go.

"Wait," I called. "Who are you—or, should I be asking, who *were* you?"

"My name," the specter replied, "is Matisse."

Matisse? I thought. *My goodness!*

I knew who Henri Matisse was! He was a great artist, born in France, back before the automobile was invented. A few years before his death in 1954, after enduring years of poverty and ridicule, he finally became world-famous for his daring, innovative use of color. Today, his once worthless paintings sell for millions.

I was very flattered to think that he'd dropped in on me simply to offer professional advice.

"Thank you, sir," I said politely. "Thank you very much."

The next thing I remember, sunlight was streaming through the blinds and my dog was whimpering in discomfort. Immediately, I took him outside.

"Can you believe it?" I said to him. "Matisse!"

Scribble looked up, narrowed his dark brown eyes, lifted his leg, and peed on my shoe.

All right, I'll admit it.

I suppose it's possible that I dreamed the entire thing.

An Inside Job

It was my own fault that I was late getting to the open house. My father had gone out to buy cigars. Cornelia was in the kitchen, trying unsuccessfully to operate a pressurized can of E-Z Cheez. Watching her struggle, I foolishly blurted out how Buzz does it, adding, as a nail in my coffin, "It always works for him." The resulting setback lasted more than an hour.

As the sign out front promised, the door to Jip's mother's house was unlocked. Inside, I encountered a thick atmosphere of potpourri-scented candles, department store perfume, and newly stirred house dust, the apparent handiwork of a woman identifying herself as Mrs. Gasp, a professional real estate agent. As Mrs. Gasp seemed neither famous nor dead, I took her at her word.

But this willingness did not apply to what I read in the book that Mrs. Gasp instructed me to sign. On a brown collapsible card table in the entry was a padded plastic-covered visitor log, uncomfortably similar to the guest register I'd signed at Jip's funeral. According to this evidence, somehow, in the time between Mrs. Gasp's unlocking of the front door and my arrival, Jip's mother's house had been inspected by Sam Walton, Mrs. Franklin D. Roosevelt, and Nathaniel 'King' Cole, plus a family group identified as the Thompsons of Niles, Michigan.

Frankly, I doubted it.

Something about Mrs. Gasp's glib manner and flamboyant taste in silk scarves told me she was the sort of person who would pad the log in order to make prospective buyers think they'd better make an offer right away. Of course, I'm sure she also had doubts about me, being only a boy, unaccompanied by house-hunting adults, and inadvertently signing my name, "Lawson, Lawson, Lawson, Lawson, Hey, Where've You Been So Long, Lawson."

"Thanks anyway," I said, when Mrs. Gasp offered to show me around. "I'm just looking."

I was disappointed to discover that my ghost goo wasn't where I'd left it in the bathroom. Perhaps Mrs. Gasp had tidied up. I made a mental note to check the trash later, after I'd searched the basement. According to the ghost of Nat 'King' Cole, I was looking for a brown metal box.

Like being under water, or in outer space, being in an empty basement in the middle of the afternoon can play tricks on your senses. It's not just that it's dark, it's that all of the sounds from above are amplified.

A person walking on the floor upstairs goes *tap-tap-tap*, like rhythm sticks or a snare drum. A dropped object sounds like a rifle shot. A toilet flushing becomes Victoria Falls.

On the other hand, voices seem to be passed through a sieve, with the upper ranges separated out and only the deeper, more bass tones getting through. Conversations from above are transmitted in fragments, and often these are unintelligible.

I couldn't be certain, but it sounded to me as if Mrs. Gasp was showing Jip's mother's house to the Japanese emperor, or possibly to his official representative. Whoever the man was, he was taking his time with the rooms upstairs, and for that I was grateful.

Jip's mother's basement had bare concrete walls, a sloping concrete floor with a perforated drain cover, and a ceiling that's actually the subfloor and support joists for the house upstairs. The whole thing was a big empty cavern—dark, dusty, damp, and smelling like yesterday's socks. As far as I could see, there was no place to hide anything.

But I had to ask myself: *Why would the ghost of Nat 'King' Cole lie to me?*

Since I didn't know exactly what I looking for, I decided to approach the problem as a trained archaeologist excavating an ancient city would. What this requires, I had read somewhere, is the application of the grid method, a technique in which you divide the area into equal squares and carefully search one square at a time.

In the field, archaeologists use string and stakes to mark off the grid. Unfortunately, I hadn't thought to bring string or stakes with me, but as it turns out it was just as well, since a concrete slab doesn't lend itself to stake pounding. Chalk would have helped, but I hadn't brought that either, so what I wound up doing was scratching a wiggly checkerboard on the floor with a piece of gravel I found in the window well.

Forty-five minutes later, after a few frantic false alarms set off by footsteps upstairs, I'd completed my examination of the basement, turning up seventeen spiders, sixty-three roly-polies, five cockroaches, ten daddy longlegs, nine beetles, a dried worm, countless mouse droppings, four nails, a brass screw, a jar lid, eighteen inches of multicolored wire, a water-stained receipt for cypress mulch, a lump of fiberglass insulation, a shiny triangle of galvanized ductwork that cut my finger when I picked it up, a mildewed Yu-Gi-Oh trading card, and a plastic token from a board game, either Sorry or Parcheesi.

Was I disappointed? You bet.

Suddenly, light streamed down from the house above.

"The basement offers such possibilities," Mrs. Gasp was saying, her high-heeled shoes clacking on the stairs. "Although it isn't finished, with a minimum of effort it could become a bedroom, a home theater, a workshop, an office suite, or in your case perhaps a rehearsal room."

Uh-oh, I thought. *And me without my ghost goo!*

Adopting the tree-hiding technique of the three-toed sloth, I hung upside down from the basement ceiling, my hands and feet gripping the rafters.

"That's okay," her prospective client replied. "I've seen all I need to see."

Whew! I thought.

My fingers ached. My ankles throbbed. My body's blood supply rushed to fill my brain. Nevertheless, I was prepared to remain in this unnatural position until the coast was clear. And although this gymnastic feat was inspired by one of earth's most feeble-minded mammals, as it turned out it was the smartest thing I could have done.

I found what I was looking for.

Roughly two feet higher than my head, just below the floor above, a narrow ledge runs the perimeter of Jip's mother's basement. It's here, at intervals of six feet, that the wood-frame house is bolted to its concrete foundation. And it was in the perpetual shadow of this rough shelf, hidden beside a laminated rim joist, that I spied a small brown strongbox.

Eureka! I thought, traveling arm over arm to my quarry, like Spiderman rushing to a rescue. *I've got it!*

Not so fast, fate replied.

The box was heavier than it looked. Although measuring only fourteen inches by ten inches by six inches—slightly larger than a lunch box—it weighed as much as a full-grown Jack Russell terrier. When my fatigued fingers wrapped around the plastic handle, the unexpected weight of the strongbox's fire-, flood-, and theft-resistant construction forced me to drop it, followed immediately by my own unfortunate self.

A seventeen-pound strongbox hitting a concrete floor makes a distinctive *wham!* sound.

A one-hundred-and-fifteen-pound boy hitting a concrete floor goes, *Whoomp! Thud!* "Yow! Dang!"

Together, they're enough to wake the dead.

"Lawson," Mrs. Roosevelt said, appearing at my side in a semitransparent state, like the murder victim in

Topper Returns, the exasperated tone of her voice offset by her humanitarian helping hand, "let's try not to make this any harder than it needs to be."

"Yes, ma'am," I replied meekly, as she disappeared.

"Who's down there?" a voice from upstairs demanded.

I knew that voice.

It wasn't Mrs. Gasp. Nor was it some family from Michigan passing a Sunday afternoon by looking at other people's houses. No, this person and I had crossed paths before. This voice belonged to Jip's favorite cousin, and my archnemesis, Chuck!

"Oh, it's you, Lawson," he said. "What are you doing down here? And where'd you get the box?"

Chuck is one of those people who are too confident for words. Whatever he goes after, you get the feeling that he thinks he's entitled to it. Chuck will probably grow up to become a United States senator, given his good looks, his money, and his extraordinarily high regard for himself. For the moment, however, I placed him in a category previously reserved for mosquitoes, ticks, and fleas: that is, a nuisance to be gotten rid of as soon as possible.

"I was just leaving," I announced, limping toward the stairs.

"Okay, sure," Chuck replied. "But you haven't answered my question about the box."

"The box?" I asked.

"The one in your hand," Chuck clarified, pointing like a prosecutor in a courtroom. "The little brown strong-box."

"Oh," I replied, nodding. "You mean this box. It's just fireworks."

"Fireworks?" Chuck responded, clearly skeptical, his arms folded menacingly across his chest. "Explain yourself, Lawson . . ."

"Lady fingers, black cats, Roman candles, Chinese spinners, bottle rockets, cherry bombs, smoke bombs, sparklers, shooting towers, concussion devices, and various launchable incineraries—you know, the usual stuff for the Fourth of July," I improvised. "My parents don't approve, so Jip let me keep the stuff here, where it's cool and dark."

"I see," Chuck said, still disbelieving.

"Look, Chuck," I continued. "I'd love to stay and chat, but I have to get back to my dog."

I placed my foot on the stairs.

"You'd better not be lying, Lawson," Chuck said.

But lying was exactly what I was doing.

Was it wrong?

Probably.

Was I sorry?

Not much.

Whatever was inside the box, I was pretty sure that Jip wanted me to have it. And where ghosts and their gifts are concerned, I told myself, the morality of mortals fades to shades of gray.

"Just remember," Chuck warned, "I'll be watching you."

With that, Jip's athletic cousin reached into his pocket

and removed a small cylinder, flipping it up into the air with his thumb and snatching it one-handed on its descent, like the coin toss that marks the start of a football game. With a sly, icy grin, Chuck opened his palm, revealing the object in his hand: Equate brand spectral essence.

Dang! I thought. *Wouldn't you know it?*

Of all the people to find my ghost goo!

The Mystery Box

When you think about it, a strongbox is a strange sort of invention.

Although it's made like a safe, it's as portable as a briefcase, so if somebody else wants it he can swipe it without much trouble. What he can't easily do, however, is open it, because a strongbox is built to keep unauthorized persons out.

The one I was looking at was a Sentinel Ultra 75, a titanium-clad, ceramic-lined container with a carbonized handle and a pick-proof, U.S. military–issue, four-digit lock. Jip's casket wasn't built to standards as high as this. Against such high-tech protection, power tools and hand axes would break in half. Explosives would merely leave a residue. So unless you have the means to slather it with ghost goo, the only way to get inside a Sentinel Ultra 75 is to know the combination.

The way I figured it, if you started with 0-0-0-0, then

tried 0-0-0-1, 0-0-0-2, and so on, you could attempt as many as ten thousand different sequences before you got lucky. Say you could spin three of these every minute, then, taking time out for eating, going to the bathroom, sleeping, and responding to routine interruptions, it could be a week before you got the strongbox open.

Eventually, you could do it, of course, if you were patient and made no mistakes, but somewhere along the way you'd be hoping to find a shortcut.

I wanted a shortcut now.

The first numbers I tried were the month, day, and year I was born. When this didn't work, I put in Jip's birthday. Again, no luck. I tried variations on Jip's street address, and mine, the final four digits of our telephone numbers, and our initials converted to numbers (with "J" being 10, for example, and "P" being 16). Each time, the lock held fast.

I shook the strongbox to assure myself that it wasn't empty. In response I heard a soft dull thump.

Something was in there. But what?

In the midst of this frustrating exercise, Scribble roused himself from a nap, stretched, yawned, shook his head, and ambled over to see what I was doing. He sniffed the strongbox as he'd sniff a bush hiding a rabbit.

"*Grrr!*" he said.

"What is it, Scribble?" I asked him. "Can you tell me? Use your x-ray vision."

Scribble lay on his belly on the floor, his furry legs extended front and rear, whimpering softly.

"Man, oh, man, Scribble," I said. "How I wish you could talk."

Blindly, I tried other important dates in history: the Battle of Hastings, Lindbergh's solo flight to Paris, the theatrical release of *Gone With the Wind,* Elvis's debut on *The Ed Sullivan Show,* the resignation of President Richard Nixon, the creation in Cleveland, Ohio, in 1972, of the original designs for the McDonald's Happy Meal.

The strongbox ignored each of these.

"Well, this is a fine how-do-you-do," I said to a clearly uninterested Scribble. "So close, and yet, so far."

Frustrated, I spun numbers randomly. Then I stood up and repeated the words that dog owners throughout the world speak whenever their problems become too great.

"C'mon, boy," I said. "Let's go for a walk."

Two things kept me awake that night.

One was Scribble's rawhide bone, which he'd gnawed into fragments in the bed. Some of the pieces were pulverized as small as particles of sand. Others were hard and sharp, like pottery shards. But as uncomfortable as this made my bed, it was the secret of the Sentinel Ultra 75 that had my mind tossing and turning.

Why, I pondered, *would Jip direct me to a locked box without providing the combination?*

It made no sense. Jip was my friend, not my tormentor.

What am I overlooking? I wondered.

I figured it had to be something that might be farfetched to me but to her way of thinking seemed obvious.

What I needed to do was think like Jip—a tall order. Jip's mind was her most attractive feature. Original. Unpredictable. Always entertaining.

The solution to this one, I thought, as the ceiling fan hummed, *could be right under my nose.*

Just as this idea was passing through my head, Scribble rolled over in his sleep and put his paw on my shoulder, his nose touching mine in a gentle Eskimo kiss.

"Huh, heh, huh, heh, heh," he laughed softly.

"What are you dreaming about?" I whispered, nuzzling the scruffy fur on his neck.

Once again, it was apparent that my pint-size soul mate was in need of a bath, a groggy half-thought that vanished into the night with the owl's soft call.

Back to School

"Your dog is a menace!" Cornelia was shouting.

Scribble had been caught red-handed chewing the tassels off an expensive Persian rug.

"Either get that little monster trained," Cornelia demanded, "or somebody's going to have to go!"

My father shot me a knowing look.

That afternoon, Scribble and I were en route to an afternoon make-up session of dog school. I didn't expect anything to come of it, of course. By now, Scribble's personality and habits were well established. But the gesture made a difference to my mother, and besides, apart from my new career in safe-cracking, which was not going well, I had nothing else planned for the entire summer.

Since these pages constitute a memoir, I should point out that there are many differences between what you find in novels and books about real life. For one thing, novels confine themselves to a handful of characters, so as not to overtax the reader. In novels, these characters are usually connected to one other in some imaginative way.

Real life, on the other hand, offers an endless succession of strangers, many whose names are never known, and most of whom have absolutely no connection with one another, except perhaps as a result of a chance encounter.

Novels, then, aspiring to be art, are like a painting, colorful, even dazzling in the hands of a master—such as Henri Matisse—but they're forced to live within the obvious limitations of the canvas.

Real life runs rampant. It bursts through barriers, leaps off the page, forgets where it's been, dashes off in a thousand different directions.

Real life knows no rules.

So the reader will forgive me when I tell you that the dog school instructor was someone new, a woman, well into her middle years, who, somewhere in her genetic past, appeared to have a Native American heritage. Her method for commanding the attention of the dogs was a violin, which she employed as other trainers might use a whistle. Her name, she informed the class, was Jana Jae. She claimed to be a friend of the owner.

"Would that be Frank or Sam?" I asked.

"I like to call him Mr. Walton," she admitted.

Now we're getting somewhere, I thought.

Only two other dogs were in attendance, a small white bichon frisé owned by a Chinese-American woman named Mrs. Tan, and, to Scribble's considerable delight, his friend Lady Osborne, was under the control of a girl named Ellie.

Ellie was wearing a soccer uniform, a shimmering green outfit with bright yellow stripes. She had fine, shoulder-length blond hair, a button nose, and a toothy, heart-shaped smile that brought to mind small burrowing animals, or at least their cartoon counterparts. She was noticeably sweaty, as if she'd just come from the practice field.

"I thought Lady Osborne was owned by a guy named Jeff," I said.

"He's my uncle," she replied.

"No kidding," I said.

"Well, okay," Ellie responded with a grimace. "Actually, he's my half brother, but I tell people he's my uncle because it's easier than explaining."

"Families," I said knowingly.

"Exactly," she replied.

Meanwhile, Jana Jae scratched out a tune on her fiddle, and Scribble and Lady Osborne tumbled up and down the floor like ferrets.

"Those two seem quite fond of each other," I observed.

"Well, sure they are," Ellie answered. "They're dogs.

What do they know about relationships?"

I wasn't clear about what Ellie meant. Was she saying that dogs are too trusting? That they're stupid? That they live in another world? Or was her remark an oblique way to suggest that human affection is doomed to disappointment?

Probing for the answer, I looked Ellie in the eye, and that's when it happened: a jolt, a lightning bolt, a sudden electrical connection, a fourth-dimensional *WHAM!* out of the blue, except that Ellie's eyes, like Scribble's, were brown—big and round and brown, unblinking, brown, and knowing, and when she looked at me with those big brown eyes, she looked all the way through me, as if I was the one in this narrative who was semitransparent.

Holy smokes! I thought, squirming. *What the heck was that?*

But before I could analyze the phenomenon, Jana Jae put her instrument aside and announced a parade, a three-dog leash-training exercise that concluded the class.

"Well," I said when it was over, "see you."

"Maybe," Ellie replied.

Later, I felt terrible, as if I'd done something wrong. As if I'd betrayed the memory—no, not the memory—the *presence* of Jip.

That evening, with daylight hanging around as long as possible, Scribble and I walked all the way to the cemetery to make amends.

As a place to play, Pleasant Ridge has a number of obvious drawbacks, but at least it's a fenced yard. With evening approaching, the swallows were out in force, skimming the grass for insects, gliding past Scribble at eye level, dive-bombing his head, daring him to give chase.

I unhooked his leash.

"Listen, Jip," I said softly, "I've been going through kind of a rough time."

What am I saying? I thought. *Nobody had a rougher time than Jip.*

Darting in and out of tombstones, Scribble leapt into the air, snapping at swallows. He was every bit as quick as the jet-powered birds and would have caught one, I'm sure, if he could fly.

"What I mean, Jip," I continued, "is that I don't know what I'm supposed to be doing. Can you find a way to show me?"

For reasons of her own, Jip chose to remain silent. Nor was there any intercession from Mrs. Franklin D. Roosevelt, Nat 'King' Cole, or Sam Walton, or any other ectoplasmic figure who'd been drifting around my so-called life. Unlike what I'd come to expect, particularly in a place inhabited exclusively by the dead, this evening at Pleasant Ridge, Scribble and I were alone.

In a back corner, we came across a mountain of dirt, ten or twelve feet high, rounded mound sprouting gangly, broad-leafed weeds, a man-made hill created by the left-over dirt from graves. Dislodging clods as he went, Scribble bounded to the top and wagged his tail—a mountain climber unfurling a flag.

"Come down, Scribble," I said.

As always, the little black-spotted terrier ignored my order.

Why am I feeling so guilty about my conversation with Ellie? I wondered.

It wasn't as if there'd been anything to it.

Besides, Jip was dead.

Wasn't she?

It was a question that no living person could answer.

The sun slipped toward the horizon. A soft, gold light formed an outline around Scribble, who was proudly commanding his mountain peak. An indigo bunting, a small blue finch, flitted onto a weathered tombstone and twittered to an unseen mate.

"Jip," I vowed to the breeze, "I won't let you down. You can count on me."

From his command post on the dirt pile, Scribble gave the appearance of a naturally born top dog—a fine-looking animal, so brave, so loyal, so smart.

There are sixty million dogs in America, I thought. *Is it possible that mine's the very best one?*

His legs planted firmly, Scribble sniffed the air, then the earth. Then, laying his head on the ground, he flipped onto his back and began to roll ecstatically in stink.

"Scribble!" I shouted. "Stop that!"

But Scribble is his own dog and abides by his own counsel.

The walk home was long and lonely. The sun slipped below the horizon with a brief burst of color straight from Matisse's tube before it faded into gloomy night.

Two police cars were parked at the curb when we arrived, which initially gave me a start until I heard the all-too-familiar shouting upstairs. Cornelia and Buzz had ratcheted up their long-standing disagreement.

Nothing for me to be concerned about, I told myself. *Just another story for the neighbors.*

Although the need was pressing, I was too tired to bathe my dog or myself. Together, smelling of our planet's unseemly side, we flopped to the bed without bothering to turn back the covers, thankful that the day was done. I considered trying a few more numbers on Jip's strongbox, but just the thought of doing this was like counting sheep.

I'm not sure what it was that roused me. Certainly there's nothing unusual about my waking in the middle of the night. This time, however, it wasn't Scribble's fault, for he was still sleeping soundly. This was something else— something outside.

I peeked through the window to see a sliver of a moon hanging high in the sky. Clouds were drifting over it, giving the scene the appearance of an eclipse.

Faintly, through the low, hissing white noise of my air purifier and the omnipresent rumbling of the house's air-conditioning system came stray bits and pieces of music and laughter. Careful not to wake Scribble, I slipped on my jeans and tennis shoes and stepped outside.

Jip's mother's house was ablaze with lights. It was as if a spacecraft had landed on the lawn.

Through the uncovered windows I could see grownups talking, drinking, dancing, and laughing at one another's remarks. A few people had gathered around a piano—where had that come from?—and seated at the bench, his wide, froglike mouth open as he crooned, "I don't know why I love you like I do," was the courtly Nat 'King' Cole.

A once-famous blond-haired movie star was dancing cheek to cheek with a fast-talking Cuban bandleader from television's early days. In the next room, a beefy baseball player, once the greatest home run hitter of all time, was telling a joke to the man who invented the light bulb, who laughed too soon and missed the punch line. Over in a corner, a dead writer of adventures set in the Yukon was refilling a cocktail glass for a woman who'd disappeared in the Pacific Ocean while trying to fly her plane around the world.

At the folding table, where earlier I'd seen the real estate agent, Mrs. Gasp, the wartime emperor of Japan was dealing cards to a deceased singing cowboy, a legendary magician, and Roland Young, the man who starred in *Topper Returns*. Looking on, a young poet who'd taken her own life, looking even prettier than her photos, was accepting a light for her cigarette from a craggy-faced Native American, once the chief of the Kaw Indians, and the last of his tribe to pass away. Lying on the floor, an empty bottle of whiskey at her side, snoring loudly and ignored by everyone, was a short story writer from Mississippi, a woman who'd lived a long, productive literary life.

I knew I wouldn't find Jip in this crowd. Not tonight. This wasn't just an adult party I was witnessing. This was a gathering of adults so mature they'd been deceased for years. It was as if the ghost bus had broken down on its way to a weekend in Branson, Missouri.

Even though I was almost thirteen and understood some of what was going on, I realized I had no business here. In my opinion being famous doesn't excuse bad behavior. Nor does being dead.

As I turned to go, Nat 'King' Cole, whose voice had only mellowed with death, was singing, "I'm in the mood for love simply because you're near me."

Back home, the contrast between the fresh air outside and the fetid, skunklike smell of my room could not have been greater. My days of procrastination had resulted in an aromatic emergency. Scribble was overripe.

Quickly, I turned on the tub and nabbed the sleeping terrier from the bed. Naturally, he whipped his head around and bit me.

It's nothing personal, I reminded myself, holding my hand under the faucet. *It's just his instinct.*

What's the old saying? Let sleeping dogs lie.

Of course, whoever first said that no doubt was more tolerant of bad odors than people are in modern times. These days, thankfully, we bathe.

I laid the lather on extra thick, mixing Scribble's dog shampoo with my mother's costly lavender-scented soap. For greater detergent power, I squirted half a cup of dish-washing liquid into the water, as well as a generous shot of toilet bowl disinfectant. Health risk or not, for once in his life, this dog was going to get clean.

Once the rubbing got under way, Scribble's objections ceased. Although he's not fond of soap and water, he's crazy about any sort of massage, so to let him know that I forgave him, I used my fingertips to thoroughly work the lather into his hair, especially the thick, coarse layer on his back.

Soap, water, and cleanser on a white dog with black spots work like a flame on dried lemon juice, that magic trick known to kids the world over as "invisible writing." Hidden messages are suddenly revealed.

In the past, with Scribble in the shower, I've seen shapes appear that reminded me of faces, ancient symbols, and cartoons. This time, with my dog fully immersed and the natural oils stripped from his fur, something quite unexpected began to take shape.

A sequence of numbers.

Four single-digit numbers.

The combination to the Sentinel Ultra 75.

That Jip, I thought. *What a girl! She put it right under my nose.*

A Thousand Words

What would you do?

Would you open the box right away? After all, every-thing—all the hints, the haints, and the fourth-dimensional folderol—had been leading up to this.

Or would you wait, like saving the biggest present till last to make your birthday go on a little longer?

Frankly, I was terrified, not of some ghost or genie jumping out of the box—not after all I'd seen—but of disappointment.

I can't begin to tell you how many times I've looked forward to something only to have it let me down. This is true of holidays, prizes, parties, and absolutely anything that money can buy.

What if I opened the strongbox and discovered that its contents were a collection of worthless coins from Jip's mother's high school trip to Europe? Or mortgage papers, or finger paintings, or newspaper clippings from when Americans first walked on the moon? People do save such things, I've read.

It could be anything. Family recipes. Baby curls. Letters from a secret admirer to a person who lived in the house before Jip did.

Heck, it could even be empty. Wouldn't that be something!

Maybe I should approach this as the bomb squad would, I thought. *Take it out in the backyard and open it with a long pole.*

What did the people do who opened King Tut's tomb? Did they barge right in? Or did they think about it for a while? The ones who lived to tell the tale surely waited. After pride and greed, haste is mankind's number one downfall. Fools rush in where angels fear to tread.

I dried my dog with a towel and stared at the box.

Inside, I knew, was the answer to something. But what?

If I were a religious person, I'd take this strongbox to my head holy man and ask him to say a prayer before I opened it. The combination was of near-sacred significance—at least to me:

Zero, eight, zero, three.

The day I got my dog.

Where does a story properly begin? And at what point should it be concluded? When everything's been figured out, and all the people have partners? It may happen that way in novels, but as I've said, my story is a memoir.

Sitting on the front porch with Scribble nosing about in the bushes, I waited for the sun to come up. Just as the sky was turning into a painting by Matisse, a vast silken canopy dyed with cadmium red, violet, and ultramarine blue, I turned the tumblers on the strongbox, one digit at a time.

Zero.

Eight.

Zero.

Three.

Eureka!

Inside was a single object, and like a riddle within a riddle, it presented as much of a mystery as had the box that held it: a videotape in an unmarked white cardboard sleeve, a bulky, VHS-format cassette, once the accepted standard for home recording but now an artifact of a technology whose time had passed.

My mother was in the kitchen, trying without

success to assemble the parts of the blender.

"I hate this useless thing," she was saying.

"Where's our old video player?" I asked her. "The one that was in the basement storeroom."

"Your father has it," Cornelia replied. "He took it with him to his apartment, which is fine with me, because I hated it too. It was impossible to program."

"To his *what?*" I responded.

"Oh, that's right," she said. "We were going to tell you. Your father moved out. I'm sure it's for the best."

Holy Toledo! I thought.

"And please keep that dog out of here," she admonished. "Animals in kitchens are unsanitary."

I stared in silence at the VHS tape in my hand.

This is terrible, I thought.

What do you do with a recording that you can't play back? It's like a razor blade without a razor, a BB without a rifle, a goldfish without a bowl, a can of Spaghettios without an opener, an itch without a finger, a bicycle without—well, you get the idea.

Absent a compatible deciphering device, the wafer-thin magnetic strip of Mylar sealed inside the plastic video case was no better than invisible writing. I'd come a very long way only to be disappointed.

It was becoming my personal motto: *Now what do I do?*

Nothing comes easy. You work for every foothold you secure. If anything can be guaranteed, it's setbacks.

Except for that, it's an ongoing struggle against the odds.

Where do you go for obsolete audiovisual equipment? School.

Schools are always having to make do with leftovers, repairables, and the previous decade's castoffs. (Case in point? My social studies book. Need another? Take a look at what passes for eighth grade track uniforms. How perfectly embarrassing!) The problem here, however, was that my school was closed for the summer and I couldn't wait until fall.

Then I remembered what I've always known: if you're looking for something unfashionable or outmoded at a bargain price, look no further than Wal-Mart. Not only will they have it, or something resembling it, but your satisfaction, within reason, is guaranteed.

I figured if I wasn't picky about the brand and was willing to compromise on quality, features, design, and country of origin, I could pick up a VHS player at Wal-Mart for under thirty dollars.

If I had thirty dollars.

Dang! I thought. *It's always something!*

Once again feeling sorry for myself, I put my head in my hands and let out a soft, exasperated whistle.

"Arf," Scribble responded, standing up on his hind legs and twirling like a decoration on a Bavarian music box. "Arf, arf, arf!"

"Ha!" I laughed, instantly snapping out of my funk and clapping my hands together, an action that had the immediate effect of breaking Scribble's hypnotic spell.

"You crack me up, Scribble," I said. "Honestly, sometimes I think you must be the world's funniest dog."

Beaming at the praise, the terrier sidled over and licked my hand, choosing the very spot he'd bitten only hours before.

Hmmm, I thought. *World's funniest dog.*

People pay good money to see less interesting things. Where could I find people who'd pay to see a little dog dance?

It's astonishing to me that so many of life's thorniest questions can be answered with the same two syllables:

Wal-Mart.

Within any given weekday hour, the number of people who pass through Wal-Mart's automatic sliding glass doors exceeds the total population of West Virginia, Rhode Island, Utah, and Wyoming, or so I'm led to believe. On Saturdays and Sundays, we're talking the total head count in Pennsylvania, Michigan, Ohio, and Illinois—numbers like that.

Given this kind of traffic, a performing dog, particularly a cute, freshly bathed one, could collect the necessary funds in a matter of minutes, before the store manager ever got wise.

Clearly, I'd come up with the perfect plan!

Heck, I thought, *if this works, I might just turn it into a full-time career.*

The Moviegoer

Show business isn't as easy as it looks.

For one thing, audiences are fickle. Whoever's in vogue one minute can be a has-been the next. For another, over the years, your average person has seen so much amazing stuff on TV for free that he or she is reluctant to pay for genuine live entertainment, no matter how unusual it promises to be.

Scribble and I sat out on the drool- and gum-covered sidewalk at the Wal-Mart Supercenter for nearly seven hours. It was hot, he hated it, and I had to keep putting the paltry dimes and quarters we received into the Sam's American Choice soda machine. It was the hardest work I've ever done, and I wouldn't be at all surprised if Scribble never forgives me.

Anyway, eventually we reached our financial goal, but not until I'd bought a poster board and markers and created a sign reading, SEE THE AMAZING DANCING DOG! BALL-ROOM. BALLET. TAP. JAZZ. DONATIONS ACCEPTED.

If I'd been set up to take credit cards, I could have cut the time in half.

The videotape player we bought was no bigger than a toaster oven and weighed the same as a pack of light bulbs. It had been assembled in Surinam from parts manufactured in Samoa and recycled in Tibet. The final cost with tax was $27.76. I used the change to buy a can of salted peanuts.

Cornelia was on the phone with my father when we got home.

"How dare you take the soup ladle!" she was shouting. "It was a wedding gift from my mother!"

I locked the door to my room, plugged in the player, and turned off the lights. The TV screen flickered blue, then went blank for a moment, until a white hand-written title card appeared on the screen, while a slightly warped recording of a popular song swelled underneath:

Jennifer Iris Palmer. What's So Good About Goodbye?

Scribble sat up, striking the pose of the dog in the once-famous RCA symbol.

Oh, my! I thought as my heart beat faster. *It's her funeral video.*

Suddenly, my thoughts raced back to another time.

When the news came that Jip had died, I was working on a story about a cat. The story was important to me because I planned to enter it into the Young Authors competition at school.

It was a Saturday morning, and, technically speaking, one day past the deadline for entries, but Miss Squirrel-berg, the communication arts teacher in charge of the contest, had granted me an extra weekend as a special favor. As it turned out, she needn't have bothered. I didn't win. A more punctual classmate, a vacant-faced girl whose subject was angels, did.

Frankly, I think the judging was heavily influenced by Jip's funeral. It was a ceremony that changed the way a lot of people looked at things.

I'd never been to a funeral, and despite our close ties, I almost didn't get to go to Jip's. My mother told my father that a funeral was no place for children.

"Try explaining that to Jip," Buzz said. "She'll be there. Besides, death is a natural part of life."

"No, it isn't," Cornelia insisted. "It's the opposite of life."

In the end, I decided for myself. I told my parents that since Jip had been my friend for such a long time, as sad as the occasion was, it would be wrong to miss it.

"All right," Cornelia agreed. "But we'll sit in the back. There's no need for a child to look at the body."

From the outside, the funeral home could have been a real estate office or a bank, but inside it resembled a church, with soft lights, deep carpets, and two long rows of wooden pews.

A photograph of Jip had been propped up on an easel by the table where guests signed in. Recorded music, the kind you hear in department stores, was playing softly through hidden speakers. A man with a camcorder was walking around taping everything. This, apparently, was the videotape I was watching now. I saw myself slide into a pew on the left-hand side, more than halfway back. The place was filling up fast.

I was wedged in between my parents. Next to Cornelia was a classmate, Kevin Kidman, who was with his mother and little brother, a thumb sucker in need of a nap. Next to them was Harry Fielding's mother, who for some reason had decided not to bring Harry. She was sitting with Mrs. Sutton, who'd brought all three of her giggly, look-alike daughters. It was a tight fit.

Mrs. Fielding told Mrs. Kidman that she'd had a hard time deciding to come.

"I remember going to my grandmother's funeral when I was seven or eight years old," I recall Mrs. Fielding saying. "I stood on tiptoes and looked at her in that exquisite velvet-lined casket. It was like she was shut up in a jewelry box and couldn't get out. The second I got home, I threw my jewelry box in the trash. To this day, the sight of a jewelry box gives me the willies."

Mrs. Kidman replied that she had lost her father several years before but was sure that he continued to drop in from time to time, making noises in the middle of the night to let her know that he was okay.

"There's so much more to it than the part we can see," Mrs. Kidman said.

Too true. From where I sat, all I could see was the backs of people's heads. I had to consult Buzz's program to figure out what was going on. For some reason, even though it was a kid who was the guest of honor, the ushers had given the orchid-colored handout only to adults.

The program was created on an office copy machine and folded into a four-page flier. On the cover was a picture drawn by Jip as her days had come to a close. It showed two people, a man and a girl, one behind the other, smiling and waving, like you'd wave to a camera while vacationing at the beach. In neatly printed handwritten letters were the words, "God and me in Heaven."

This had come as a shock. Jip had never mentioned God to me. Only ghosts.

In the video, there was a shaky close-up of the program in someone's hand. Then the camera followed Mrs. Sutton and her daughters as they returned to their seats. To one side, Cornelia appeared to be admonishing Buzz, who'd cast his eyes toward the ceiling. Mrs. Sutton was whispering to Mrs. Kidman.

"She looks so beautiful," Mrs. Sutton had said. "Much better than when she was alive."

Suddenly, Scribble barked as loudly as I've ever heard him. I looked up from the video to see that Chuck was in my room.

"How did you get in?" I asked.

"How do you think?" he replied with a sneer, tossing me the empty tin of ghost goo.

Instinctively, I reached out to catch it, an action that left my face unprotected from what came next. Assuming the stance of a trained kung fu fighter, Chuck waved his hands in circles and kicked his sneaker-clad foot into the air.

I'm not a fighter. It's not that I don't believe in it; it's that I've never encountered a situation in which I thought it would improve things. Whether fighting is conducted with words, hands, weapons, or, in Scribble's case, hard, sharp teeth, it seems to me that it only drives the combatants further apart. In the long run, when the dust settles, even the winners wind up losing.

141

On this particular issue, I'm confident that Sam Walton and Eleanor Roosevelt agree with me.

Why?

Because Sam Walton grabbed Chuck by the airborne foot and flipped him onto his back, while Eleanor Roosevelt, still wearing her fur, sat her aristocratic hind end down on Chuck's chest, pinning him to the floor.

"Hey, no fair!" Chuck shouted.

"Shut up and be still!" Mrs. Roosevelt commanded.

"That's the God's honest truth," Sam Walton added.

"This thing's got a ways to go," I explained to my rescuers, referring to Jip's video.

"Okay, okay," Chuck whined. "As long as you understand that it's family property. You're not entitled to keep it."

"Message received," I said. "But keep away from the dog. He bites."

"*Grrr,*" Scribble said.

Meanwhile, the funeral video continued to play. Suddenly, the image wobbled and tilted on its side, as if the photographer had dropped the camera, but it turned out that he was only installing it on a tripod. When the picture righted itself, Reverend Somebody-or-other was talking with his eyes closed, after which he introduced the chaplain at the hospital.

The chaplain said she'd known Jip only for a couple of days, but she could tell right away that Jip was an exceptional person. Then she relayed how one night she'd been in the hospital cafeteria eating a cheeseburger when she heard a voice instructing her to go to Jip's room. Nobody else was in the cafeteria, the chaplain explained, and it wasn't the hospital intercom, nor her pager, nor her cell phone, so she figured she must be hearing things, and she went back to eating her cheeseburger. But the voice wouldn't stop calling, so finally the chaplain threw the cheeseburger into the trash and took the elevator to Jip's room. Just as she walked through the doorway, Jip died.

"I'm sure that the voice I heard that night in the cafeteria was the voice of Jennifer Palmer," the chaplain announced.

The mourners became quiet. The only sound coming from the video was the hiss of the tape going through the machine. Then, from somewhere off camera, somebody called out, "Amen." Other voices picked up the refrain. It moved like an echo around the room.

The chaplain's story was a tough act to follow, but somebody must have known what he was doing, because the next person to stand up was Jip's stepgrandfather, a well-fed man with white hair and a huge smile. He reminded me of Santa Claus. When he spoke, sunlight streamed through colored glass panels of the funeral home onto the side of his well-tanned face.

"Jip's mother told me this is a celebration, so I came to celebrate," he announced.

He held up a picture, explaining that Jip had drawn it

143

for his eighty-second birthday. He said it was a picture of him and Jip, but to me it looked like the picture on the cover of the program, the one of Jip and God.

Miss Squirrelberg, the teacher, was next. Obviously unaccustomed to performing at occasions like this, she stepped to the microphone with a sheet of notebook paper in trembling hands and began to deliver an essay in a squeaky, halting voice. It was then that I realized I'd been granted an extension for the Young Authors competition not because I was a favored student but because Miss Squirrelberg had been preoccupied with other, more awesome duties.

Other testimonials followed, most of them optimistic about the life to come, some suggesting a connection between Jip and astronomy, and one, delivered in verse, that remained unfinished when the speaker succumbed to tears.

There was a touching musical number involving Jip's classmates, and a long address by a visiting minister who talked of kingdoms and crowns. Then, finally, came the part I was hoping to see.

When I'd attended Jip's funeral, seated near the back of the room between the warring worlds of Buzz and Cornelia, most of what was happening was blocked from view. Now, with Scribble, Sam Walton, Mrs. Roosevelt, and Jip's cousin Chuck joining me, I had a front-row seat.

The lights dimmed and two somber funeral home employees dressed in suits and ties rolled out a squeaky cart on which a bulky television sat tethered to the socket by a long orange extension cord, the kind you might use when edging your sidewalk with a Weed Eater. After a few awkward moments of trial and error with the controls, they managed to get the prerecorded show under way.

"Oh, yeah," Chuck said, gasping from the weight of the determined Mrs. Roosevelt, "I remember this part."

"Y'all hush, now," Sam Walton ordered Chuck. "Don't speak 'less y'all are spoken to."

Scribble, who'd dozed off at my feet for much of the video, once again took notice of what was happening on the screen.

Set to Nat 'King' Cole's landmark 1951 recording of "Unforgettable," the sequence began with a faded snapshot of Jip as a newborn. Every few seconds, the photograph would be replaced with another one in which Jip became progressively older. By the sixth or seventh picture, the changes were no longer keeping time with the music.

I saw Jip as a baby, a toddler, and a little girl, growing up in a household that, except for the occasional change in the identity of the father, looked just like everybody else's—ordinary people with their hair messed up, eating cereal from a box, playing in a lawn sprinkler, and lying in bed in their underwear.

I felt very strange watching these images of Jip go by. It was as if this time I really was peeking through her windows.

145

It also struck me that I was seeing an image on my TV that was a recording of an image on the funeral home TV that, in turn, had been videotaped from a snapshot of a person as she appeared through a camera years before.

How far removed from real life is that?

Abruptly, the sequence switched from still pictures to a full-motion videotape, presumably the only one ever made of Jip, shot from a distance in the breezeway of a beachside motel on a family vacation.

Alone, Jip was dancing in and out of shafts of sunlight that streamed through open archways between a double row of columns, using her own invented ballet steps, bending at the waist, raising her arms into a circle around her head, bowing, reaching upward, twirling, and skipping as girls do so well. She appeared neither sad nor happy, but intent on what she was doing, mastering a silent, enchanted language that even from such a great distance spoke directly to me.

"See there, Scribble," I whispered reverently. "That's how it's done."

At last, I knew exactly what Jip looked like. Methodically, I committed the placement of each detail to memory: eyes here, nose there, smile like that, muscles in her face working together just so, freckles, hair, ears, tilt of head, roundness of cheek, awkward step, graceful arms, long, fluid fingers—I put it all together and the picture was unique. Jip was truly one of a kind. And now, her image was fixed forever in my mind.

Complete.

Permanent.

Unforgettable.

I removed the tape from the player and handed it to Chuck.

"Thanks," I said.

"Yeah, sure," Chuck replied, as Mrs. Roosevelt stood up. "Whatever."

Scribble

Scribble is a great dog. Sometimes, when I'm reading a book, he'll climb up and lie down in my lap, waiting patiently until I'm done. He wrestles with me, plays ball, watches television, eats the same food I eat.

Scribble never has what's euphemistically called an "accident" in my aunt and uncle's house, which is where I live now. No matter what the weather, he's always ready for a walk. He chases rabbits, but only until they disappear into the brush. He can sniff out mice, earthworms, and buried bones. Once, just as I was coming home from school, he caught the rooster by its long tail feathers.

My aunt got to him just in time.

"I told you, no chickens!" she shouted.

But since it was the rooster Scribble had run down, while staying away from the hens, he may have thought he had her on a technicality.

Scribble's very fond of children and dogs. When he barks, it's urgent news, and when he bites me, he's always got a good reason. Scribble still keeps odd hours, to be sure, but it's at odd hours that the most interesting things happen.

I can't imagine life without Scribble. That he started out as Jip's dog is important, but it's no longer the most important thing. I love him for who he is, not whom he once belonged to.

On the other hand, although I realize it sounds disloyal, I'm becoming accustomed to life without my parents. I see Buzz infrequently—perhaps once every three or four weeks—at his apartment, where there isn't much to do. It's small, dark, and filled with blue cigar smoke.

My mother still lives in our house and struggles to operate the appliances.

Once, when I was back home, I saw Ellie. She was with a group of girls buying makeup at Wal-Mart. She giggled, waved to me, then turned away. I don't know where her half brother's dog was.

The ghosts have gone, back to wherever such life forms belong, if *life form* is the proper term for those who've passed on. Except for an occasional encounter with Sam Walton working at various positions in his place of business, I haven't seen hide nor hair of the spirits since their party at Jip's mother's house.

Speaking of parties, tomorrow is my thirteenth birthday. When I look in the mirror, I can see that I've aged considerably, as Scribble did when he was in the company of Mrs. Roosevelt—not to mention that I've outgrown my clothes.

I plan to celebrate all day long, with my dog.

As I write this, he comes over and licks my face. His breath is warm. His ears are velvet soft. His chin whiskers tickle.

I wonder: Does he think he's a person?

Or does he take me for a dog?

WITHDRAWN FROM
ALBANY PUBLIC LIBRARY-MAIN
ALBANY, N. Y.